Blast From the Present

Slocum turned back to the mouth of the mine and saw a glint of light reflecting off a blue gun barrel. It was certain death if he tried to leave.

A bullet sang off a wall to Slocum's right. He flinched and crouched. Two more shots followed in the span of a heartbeat. Without a choice, he inched back into the mine, then bolted and ran as hard as he could . . .

Another shot lent speed to his retreat. He heard the hissing fuse. He had no idea how long it had been lit. Slocum went pale when he saw how close the fuse was to burning down to the blasting cap.

Slocum dived and clawed at the now burned fuse. His fingers clamped down over the sizzling spark marching inexorably for the blasting cap and four sticks of dynamite.

The magnesium in the fuse burned his fingers, but he yanked back and pulled the fuse and blasting cap away from the end stick of dynamite.

The cap detonated and knocked him backward into the wall. Then the world went black . . .

JAKE LOGAN

SLOCUM
AND THE
DYNAMITE KID

JOVE BOOKS, NEW YORK

PWES
Logan

THE BERKLEY PUBLISHING GROUP
Published by the Penguin Group
Penguin Group (USA) Inc.
375 Hudson Street, New York, New York 10014, USA

Penguin Group (Canada), 90 Eglinton Avenue East, Suite 700, Toronto, Ontario M4P 2Y3, Canada
(a division of Pearson Penguin Canada Inc.)
Penguin Books Ltd., 80 Strand, London WC2R 0RL, England
Penguin Group Ireland, 25 St. Stephen's Green, Dublin 2, Ireland (a division of Penguin Books Ltd.)
Penguin Group (Australia), 250 Camberwell Road, Camberwell, Victoria 3124, Australia
(a division of Pearson Australia Group Pty. Ltd.)
Penguin Books India Pvt. Ltd., 11 Community Centre, Panchsheel Park, New Delhi—110 017, India
Penguin Group (NZ), 67 Apollo Drive, Rosedale, North Shore 0632, New Zealand
(a division of Pearson New Zealand Ltd.)
Penguin Books (South Africa) (Pty.) Ltd., 24 Sturdee Avenue, Rosebank, Johannesburg 2196,
South Africa

Penguin Books Ltd., Registered Offices: 80 Strand, London WC2R 0RL, England

SLOCUM AND THE DYNAMITE KID

A Jove Book / published by arrangement with the author

PRINTING HISTORY
Jove edition / June 2009

Copyright © 2009 by Penguin Group (USA) Inc.
Cover illustration by Sergio Giovine.

ISBN: 978-0-515-14639-4

JOVE®
Jove Books are published by The Berkley Publishing Group,
a division of Penguin Group (USA) Inc.
375 Hudson Street, New York, New York 10014.
JOVE® is a registered trademark of Penguin Group (USA) Inc.
The "J" design is a trademark of Penguin Group (USA) Inc.

PRINTED IN THE UNITED STATES OF AMERICA

10 9 8 7 6 5 4 3 2 1

1

This was lonesome country, and John Slocum liked it that way. The whistling wind from the Wasatch Mountains cut at his leathery face, but he hardly noticed because of the damp feel to the air. The storm was nowhere to be seen, but the hints were more than enough to warn him to quit the trail from Wyoming into Utah and to find shelter. In spite of this premonition of a nasty spring thunderstorm, he kept riding.

His mare trudged along under him, tired but game to keep moving. They had been on the trail almost a month, covering long distances each day and moving ever westward. Slocum had left nothing behind him in Denver, nothing much more than three brothers intent on ventilating him, a large poker debt unlikely to be collected, and a French-woman he had scorned who had vowed to rip out his eyes and eat them. Denver had quickly become a good place to ride away from, but there hadn't been any destination in mind when he set out before dawn that day more than three weeks in the past. Wyoming barrens had flowed beneath his horse's hooves like water tumbling along in a stream. The Grand Tetons had risen slowly, day by day, to the brilliant sapphire sky, hazy and serene and magnificent, but there had been nothing to hold him there longer than it took for him to appreciate their beauty. His path had turned immediately southward and then west once more in his quest to find a trail to Salt Lake City. Nothing awaited him there either, and he would ride on after a day or two of rest. He sure as hell wasn't likely to find any saloon worth the name in a town run by Mormons.

Slocum sat a little straighter in the saddle when distant thunder rolled along behind him. The storm had formed and was coming after him. He had been mistaken about the direction, not that it mattered. In the mountains, a sudden spring storm got him just as wet coming from the east as it did from the west.

"Giddyup," he said, putting his heels to the mare's flanks to keep her moving. His horse seldom reared at the sound of gunfire, but a thunder peal spooked her. As reliable as she was, Slocum wanted to keep her calm and dry. "We've got to find a cave if we want to ride out the storm."

He looked around, but the rocky terrain didn't lend itself well to such luxuries as an empty cave. Slocum turned the horse toward a grove of pine trees, thinking to find a hollow where they could find shelter, even if the weather got bad. Ten minutes searching gave him what he desired. Tall rocks would shield the worst of the wind, and strategically placed trees would let him string his canvas sheet in such a way that both he and the horse could escape the worst of the rain. He looked up into the hills and judged that he wasn't likely to be washed off the face of the earth by a flood. This was a decent spot to outwait the storm.

He started gathering wood after tethering his horse to a low-hanging limb of a juniper tree. He had barely scraped out a fire pit when the ground shook so powerfully under his feet that it drove him to his knees. A few seconds later came the rolling thunder of a massive explosion. He scrambled to his feet and grabbed for his horse's reins. The mare had reared at the disturbance, struck the limb where the tether had been looped, and broken it off. It took Slocum a few seconds to calm the horse.

"That wasn't an avalanche," Slocum said, as much to calm himself as the mare. "There's no mining I know of around here, but that doesn't mean somebody's not blasting." He saddled his horse and packed his gear. The storm was coming, but he had to find out what had caused the explosion. A prospector might have gotten careless and might now be in need of help.

A distant crack of thunder told Slocum what else might have caused a tragedy in the mountain pass. He had heard of blasting powder being set off just before a cloudburst. Sparks sometimes danced on flagpoles to announce a coming thunderstorm, and the smartest mine supervisors always got the hell away from their magazines until the sun shone again.

"We won't be out in the rain," Slocum said, patting the horse's neck and hoping his promise wasn't a lie. The mare turned a large brown accusing eye in his direction and snorted. The horse didn't believe him. Slocum didn't believe himself either. A cold, heavy drop of rain spattered against the back of his neck. He rummaged about until he found his slicker. By the time he pulled it around his body, the first of the spring rain pelted down on him.

He could have stayed in the camp and let the approaching storm peter out in an hour or two, but it wasn't in Slocum to do that when men might be injured. Although he was just passing through and hadn't seen any indication, he doubted a railroad was being cut through this pass. No evidence of supply trains, no tracks, no sign that this trail was heavily traveled hinted at heavy construction. Even if a crew was dynamiting for a railroad bed, the explosion had been powerful enough to bring down an entire mountain.

The cloud of dust rising ahead of him in spite of the fitful rain showed where to ride. He turned his mare's face off the narrow trail and cut through more rugged territory until he reached a rise. Stretched below him were tons of strewn rock reduced to the size of gravel. The explosion had left a huge scar in the mountainside, but he saw no trace of people anywhere he looked. Slocum dismounted and crouched down to carefully study the landscape.

The only things moving in his field of vision were small animals scurrying about in the vegetation a dozen yards off and the leaves of oak trees now disturbed by the increasingly heavy rain. He pulled up his collar and settled the slicker around his shoulders and kept looking. The blast hadn't just happened naturally. He had worked in mines enough to know about pockets of explosive gases. A single drill bit entering such a pocket of "damp" created a spark that could bring down the entire mine.

Over the patter of the rain he heard a distant neighing of horses, followed closely by the creaking of wood and the clanking of chains.

"Let's go see what happened," Slocum said to his mare. Riding to the point of the explosion was a waste of time. He knew a powerful lot of dynamite had gone off. Who had set it mattered more to him than verifying that an explosion had ripped away the side of a mountain. He could see the stony remains for himself.

He skirted the debris field, found a game trail, and cut across the farthest stretch of the blasted rock to reach a double-rutted road. From the look of it, the road provided a second way through the pass, parallel to the trail he had been on prior to the explosion.

The grass alongside the road had been crushed down by several horses, and ruts in the road were already filling with rainwater. A wagon or two had passed this way recently. When he heard the neighing of a frightened horse, followed by a single gunshot, Slocum knew where they had gone. He trotted along the road, heading in the direction he had intended to ride anyway.

Less than five minutes later, he came on a pair of wagons. The axle of one wagon had broken. The other wagon canted sharply to the right side, having driven off the narrow road and gotten mired in newly churned mud. Slocum wiped the rain from his face as he studied the wagons and the people surrounding them. He counted nine people—two women, four men, and three urchins hardly old enough to walk.

One man, holding a rifle, spotted Slocum and turned in his direction. Slocum stayed where he was, watching and waiting to see if the man would open fire. Instead, he lowered the rifle and waved.

"Hello! Can you help us out?"

Slocum waited another few seconds. The man didn't put the rifle to his shoulder. Instead, he turned and handed it to a woman crowding close behind him. She had two of the small children clinging to her skirts and fearfully peering around at the stranger in the rain.

Riding slowly, he approached. The one wagon had a busted axle for sure, and the other was mired up to the hub in mud. A broad, shallow stream ran alongside the road. The rain runoff from higher in the hills had created a small floodplain that the inexperienced wagon driver had veered into. The second man grumbled under his breath as he worked in the rain to get a long tree limb under the bogged-down wagon's rear axle to help boost it from the mire. A young girl Slocum had not seen before sat in the driver's box, reins in hand and looking confused.

"You got some trouble, I see," Slocum said.

"You set off that explosion?" asked the woman now holding the rifle. She glared at him as if all this was his fault.

"No, ma'am, I didn't. I was setting up camp to ride out the storm when the ground shook. I worried that some miners might be hurt, so I went to investigate. Looked as if the whole side of the mountain just upped and blew away, but I didn't see any mine—or miners."

"Spooked our team. Broke an axle and had to put down one of the horses that broke a leg."

"Reckon I was lucky. All the blast did was frighten my mare." Slocum patted the horse's wet neck. The horse shook her head and sent water flying.

"You lend a hand? We're on our way to Sage Junction."

"Don't know the town, but if it's that way, we're likely traveling to the same spot," Slocum said.

He dismounted and checked the wagon with the broken axle.

"Unless you have a spare axle, this one's not going anywhere." This provoked hushed, angry conversation between the man and woman.

"A little help over here, would you, mister?" called the other man. He leaned on the end of the tree limb, but couldn't lever up the second wagon from the mud.

"Might be easier if you had those children fetch tree limbs and put them under the wheels every time we rock the wagon forward. That'll keep it from sinking deeper in the same hole."

The man barked orders while Slocum walked to the girl in the driver's box. She was younger than he had thought at first, hardly twelve and a mere slip of a girl.

"You an experienced driver?" Slocum asked.

She shook her head as if she didn't dare speak.

"How long have you been on the trail, you and your folks?"

"We left St. Louis over a month back. We're on our way to Salt Lake City."

"Lenore, be quiet," snapped the woman Slocum took to be the girl's mother. There was a strong resemblance in their long, straight noses and bright green eyes.

"Pilgrims?" Slocum hazarded.

"Mormons on our way to be with others of our kind," the woman said tartly. "You aren't one of those who wish us harm, are you?"

"I was enjoying the solitude, ma'am," Slocum said, "and not wishing any trouble on anyone when the blast brought me this way." He turned and joined the man he took to be her husband at the end of the lever. Together they heaved and rocked the wagon forward. The little children played at putting deadwood under the wheels by throwing the limbs into the water to make large splashes, but both women and the other man joined in. After a few minutes of effort, the wagon rattled and clanked free and rolled down the road a few yards before the girl brought the team to a halt.

"Thank you, sir," the man said. He hesitated, then thrust out his hand. Slocum shook it. "We owe you a debt of gratitude."

"Just being neighborly." Slocum wiped more of the rain from his face, but it was a losing battle now. The rain fell steadily and chilled him to the bone.

"You're 'bout the first one," said the girl in the wagon. She looked at Slocum with wide eyes and an astonished expression. The rain beat down on her head, plastering her bonnet to her hair like glue.

"Hush, Lenore," her mother said. "What she said is true. We all owe you a debt of gratitude, sir."

Slocum mopped at his face with his bandanna and looked back at the wagon with the broken axle. "What are you going to do about repairing that one?"

"We do not have the tools. We'll press on to Sage Junction, barter for a new axle, return, and fix it."

"You might want to leave a few folks here to watch over the wagon. Although I haven't seen anyone else riding this trail, anyone coming upon it would think they had found a treasure chest if it's abandoned."

The men put their heads together and argued for a spell. Slocum grew tired of their palavering, touched the tip of his hat, and said, "I'd best be moving on myself. This rain's not going to let up anytime soon."

"Would you ride along with us?" the girl said. "Just to town?"

"Lenore!"

"If you're not going to camp to ride out the storm, reckon I can do that," said Slocum. "It always pays to have someone watching out for you on the road in such bad weather."

Slocum was as cold and wet as he could get. Pressing on to Sage Junction suited him better than trying to pitch a new camp.

"It's not far," Lenore said. "Only a few miles. We can make it in a couple hours."

This decided Slocum. He rode with the Mormons into Sage Junction, and they never so much as addressed a word in his direction. The women looked at him as if he had horns poking up through the brim of his Stetson, and the man whose wagon he had helped pry loose from the mud never bothered to introduce himself. It wasn't lost on Slocum either that the man rode with a rifle by his side. The only friendly one was the young girl, and her mother sent her to the rear of the wagon. Slocum reckoned this was so he wouldn't infect her with his neighborly ways.

The town was about drowned by the time Slocum stepped down from his horse. He stretched his back and realized how long he had been in the saddle, the past several hours riding in the rain. His mare had reached the point of stumbling. If Sage Junction hadn't come up when it had, he would have left the settlers to their own devices and found himself a spot to camp. As it was, they had reached town about two hours before sundown. The storm had turned the world a dull gray, but the rain had settled down to a gentle drizzle. A new river ran from one side of the main street to the other, threatening to slosh up into shops and other buildings if the rain kept on much longer.

"Time to get you cared for," Slocum said, leading his horse to the livery stables. He dickered with the owner a while and got a reasonable deal for drying, currying, and feeding the mare something more than the grass she had been living on all across Wyoming.

He stepped out into the rain and pulled down his hat brim. The boardwalks allowed water and mud to seep up from beneath, but walking on them was better than sinking ankle deep in the muddy streets. Slocum hunted for a saloon, and found one right away with a sign as bold as brass, telling him this wasn't Mormon country. Not yet. He stood in the saloon doorway and saw how the family in the wagon worked to get everything secured. They had parked in an open lot across the street catty-corner from the saloon. They all looked miserable, but Slocum had no call to share that woe when food and a few beers awaited him inside.

The crowded room was a testament to the foul weather. Men from one end of town to the other had abandoned their chores early today to boast how their roofs leaked more—or less—than everyone else's and to generally commiserate about the bad weather.

Slocum had enough money riding in his pocket to buy two roast beef sandwiches, a pickle, and a couple beers to wash down each sandwich. When he finished, he felt half-way human again, but his clothing was still dripping onto the saloon floor.

Belly full and feeling able to whip his weight in wildcats, Slocum went to the doorway to see if the Mormons had settled down. The rain had let up, but the lot was flooded. Getting their wagon moving again would be a chore. Slocum started outside to tell them how to set their wheels to make it easier to leave in the morning, probably to return to the other wagon with a spare axle.

He stopped when he saw a woman talking earnestly with Lenore. The young girl pressed back against a building while the woman bent over so their faces were only inches apart. At first, Slocum thought the woman was giving the girl a tongue-lashing. Then, he saw her pull something from her purse. Lenore's face lit up as if the sun had come out.

This unleashed a torrent of words from the girl. She gestured and pointed and kept talking faster and faster. Slocum was curious what she was saying, but could not hear. Then he became even more interested when the woman straightened and turned so he could see her clearly. A ray of sunlight broke through the clouds and spotlighted her pale oval face.

He might have seen a lovelier woman in his day, but he

was hard-pressed to remember when or where. The best he could tell, she had bright blue eyes to go with the midnight black hair poking out from under her hat. High cheekbones, full lips that begged for a kiss, a swan's neck, and a grace in movement that made her seem as if her feet floated over the ground rather than slopping through the mud. Her gingham dress was impeccably clean, and fit her shapely body with a perfection that told of long hours of expert tailoring.

For a moment, their eyes locked. She smiled faintly, then disappeared. Slocum blinked and saw that she had simply taken a step to her right, gotten behind the building where she spoke with Lenore, and never come back.

Slocum walked along the main street, trying to catch sight of the lovely woman as she hurried along the street on the far side of the buildings. He crossed over, went to that street, and looked around. She was nowhere to be seen. Slocum walked around and asked a few merchants who had been more diligent about keeping their businesses open, but were now closing up for the day. No one had seen her.

His boot steps turned back toward the settlers' muddy camp. As he rounded the building where he had seen Lenore and the woman talking, he almost collided with the young girl.

"Please, sir," Lenore said, reaching out and pushing him away. "Don't let them see you, or I'll be in terrible trouble."

"I was just going to see your pa about how he parked his wagon. How's that going to get you into trouble?"

"You saw me talking to her. You saw what she did."

"The woman in the gingham dress?"

Lenore went pale and put her hand to her mouth. Slocum thought she was going to be sick.

"Who is she?"

"I . . . I don't know and I don't care. I should never have done it!"

"What? I won't tell your ma or pa."

"You won't?" Lenore looked somewhat relieved, but obviously thought Slocum was capable of any perfidy.

"What did she give you?"

"Candy," Lenore said, averting her eyes and looking as if she had robbed a bank. "She gave me a peppermint. My ma says that's the Devil's work. All candy is, but it's so tasty," Lenore said.

"For all his ways, the Devil doesn't have to rely on candy all that much," Slocum said, knowing how they would react to him having two beers over at the saloon. "There're lots worse things in the world than a peppermint candy."

Lenore looked up guiltily.

"I already ate it. I was going to share with my brother and sister, but I didn't want them to become the Devil's playthings."

Slocum had to laugh at that. "Smart of you."

Lenore finally decided he wasn't going to tell her parents.

"Thank you, sir. You're nowhere near as evil as my ma said."

"I don't know about that," Slocum said, remembering what he had been thinking when he spotted the woman who had been talking to Lenore. His thoughts had been decidedly impure and downright lustful. "What did she ask you?"

The answer startled Slocum.

"She wanted to know all about the explosion."

2

The rain refused to stop falling. Slocum peered out from under the roof in front of the Crazy Eights Saloon at the leaden sky. The lightning had stopped ripping apart the sky sometime in the night, but the drizzle continued unabated and turned Sage Junction into one giant hellhole of mud and ankle-deep puddles.

He pulled back to the shelter of the roof, and saw that the Mormons were wrestling an axle into the rear of the wagon. They hadn't been overly friendly, but Slocum felt obligated to turn up his collar, duck his head, and venture into the rain. The patter of drops on the brim of his hat almost drowned out the man's greeting.

"Come to see us off?"

Slocum looked up and hesitated. Then he said, "I wanted to see if you needed a hand getting the axle into the rear of your wagon. The womenfolk look to be having a time of it."

"They can cope," the man said. He glanced toward the rear where Lenore, her mother, and two of the small children struggled to slide the heavy wood rod into the rear. Without being invited, Slocum pushed past the man and helped get the axle into the rear of the wagon.

"That's a mighty heavy axle. Will it fit the other wagon?" Slocum asked. He wiped his hands off on his jeans.

"The wheelwright claims it can be made to fit," the man said.

"I'd ride back to help, but it's time I moved on," Slocum said. He looked at Lenore. Her eyes were wide and she bit her lower lip, obviously afraid he would tell her parents about speaking with the woman yesterday—and taking candy.

"We can overcome our problems," the man said.

"You ever think on what caused that explosion?"

Lenore stiffened and went pale, but neither of her parents took notice.

"Can't say I did. We had other problems to deal with after the blast. 'Twarn't nothing more than miners," the man said. "Or perhaps a railroad crew blasted to lay tracks."

Slocum doubted either of those reasons for the blast. He wished he could talk more freely to Lenore and find out more of what she had told the woman. A smile came to his lips. He wished he could find the woman. She was quite a beauty, rivaling any Southern belle Slocum had ever laid eyes on.

"Good luck. I hope this is the last of your travails getting to Salt Lake City," Slocum said.

The man stared hard at him, then came to a decision. He thrust out his hand. Slocum shook it. No words were spoken, but finally Slocum had convinced the man he meant no harm. Slocum touched the brim of his hat to the ladies and winked at Lenore. The girl almost exploded when she released her pent-up breath. She finally knew that Slocum was not going to tell her parents about her horrific transgression.

Slocum made his way back across the street, trying in vain to avoid deep puddles. The last one before he reached the shelter of the overhang in front of the Crazy Eights caused water to rise up and over the top of his boot. He flopped down in a chair and took off the boot to drain it. The

Mormons rattled from town, heading back into the hills to repair their second wagon. Slocum wished them well.

He pulled on the boot and patted his shirt pocket. He had enough money left for a final beer before riding out of Sage Junction on his way to . . . elsewhere.

Inside the saloon, he found a larger number of patrons than he expected. The rain had driven them into the relatively dry building. The barkeep had put out only three tin pots to catch drips falling from the ceiling. A couple other stores in town Slocum had visited were wetter inside than out in the rain. After the storm blew on through, somebody could make a pretty penny repairing roofs. He almost considered that since he was down to his last nickel, but there wasn't any reason for him to remain in Sage Junction.

"Beer," Slocum said, dropping the nickel so it spun about a few times on its rim before falling flat to the bar.

"You ain't goin' with them?" The barkeep pointed outside.

"You mean with the settlers? I helped them out on the trail." Slocum sipped the beer with relish, then set the mug down on the bar. "Them and me don't see eye to eye on some of life's finer things."

"You callin' my beer that? A finer thing in life?"

"Reckon so," Slocum said.

The barkeep broke out laughing. "That's about the funniest thing I ever heard. This beer's bitter enough to make a weasel puke. Since you done drained that one, let me give you another one. On the house."

This sparked interest along the bar. The man next to Slocum poked him in the ribs with an elbow and asked, "How'd you git that son of a bitch skinflint to give you a free beer? Old Morgan there's not likely to piss on his own ma if she was on fire."

"That's not true," Morgan piped up. "But I'd have to be drinkin' water and not my own brew. Wouldn't want to waste a drop of—what'd you call it, mister? The finest thing in life!"

Slocum didn't bother correcting Morgan. Instead, he lifted his full mug in a toast and worked on it. When he was almost done, a hush fell over the saloon patrons. Slocum looked up into the mirror behind the bar and saw a burly, bowlegged man come in, hold the swinging doors open for a moment, then release them so they *whup-whupped* behind him. The cowboy was dressed in a red and black checked flannel shirt, and jeans worn so thin that Slocum fancied he could see skin through the cloth. The man's boots were caked with mud, but were probably fancy and very expensive if the Spanish roweled spurs were any indication. They were silver, and clinked as he strutted over to the bar.

"Gimme some good whiskey," he said. "None of that shit you pour for these miserable peckerwoods."

"Right away," Morgan mumbled. As the barkeep passed in front of the man, he reached across the bar and grabbed Morgan by the collar. The man yanked so hard the bartender's shirt ripped.

"You call me sir or you don't call me nuthin'."

"If that goes for everyone," Slocum said, "then I'd say that *nuthin'* had better let loose right now." Slocum turned and pulled back his coat to reveal the well-used Colt Navy slung in his cross-draw holster.

"Who are you, little man?"

Slocum stayed silent. His cold green eyes fixed on the man's squinty pale eyes.

"I ain't pickin' a fight with you," the cowboy said. He released his hold on Morgan's shirt. The barkeep staggered back and rattled glasses on the back bar.

"There's no need for a fuss," Morgan said. "I'll fix you both up with a drink."

"There's no need," Slocum said. "Nuthin' is ready to leave."

"You got no call tellin' me what to do, you sack of shit!"

The cowboy went for his pistol, but Slocum was already moving. He cleared leather and the long barrel of his Colt crashed into the cowboy's wrist. The snapping bone echoed in the Crazy Eights Saloon like a gunshot. But Slocum wasn't finished. As the cowboy shrieked in pain, Slocum half turned and drove his right elbow into the man's face. With a broken wrist and a crushed nose, the cowboy staggered back. Slocum followed as surely as a wolf after its prey.

He kicked out, caught the man's boot just above the flashing silver spur, and sent him crashing to the floor. The cowboy hit so hard he broke a floorboard. Slocum stepped closer, gauged his distance, and kicked hard. The toe of his boot met the jutting chin and snapped the man's head back so hard it smashed into the floor and broke another board. The cowboy lay sprawled with a broken wrist and nose and sputtering blood.

Slocum rolled him onto his side so he wouldn't drown in his own blood, grabbed a collar, and began dragging. The cowboy was even heavier than he looked. Slocum tugged him through the swinging doors into the muddy street, where he dumped him into a mud puddle. Quite a crowd had gathered by now, including a small, wiry man with a mustache about as big as anything Slocum had seen. If this man weighed a hundred fifty pounds, the mustache was half that. The ends twitched as the man looked from the fallen cowboy to Slocum and then back.

"You done this?"

"He slipped," Slocum said, "while he was trying to beat up the barkeep."

"You roughed up Big Willie Wilson because he was givin' Morgan a hard time?"

"As I said, he slipped. A couple times. Clumsy galoot." Slocum prodded Big Willie with his toe. The man groaned and then sputtered, spitting blood and snorting a stream out both nostrils.

"Son of a gun," the man said. "Put 'er there, mister. I'm Stanford Allen."

Slocum shook his hand.

"I'm Stanford *Allen*," the man said.

"I heard you. That name supposed to mean something?"

"I own the Crazy Eights. And two other gin mills in this here town."

"Pleased to make your acquaintance." Slocum introduced himself, but noticed how everyone in the gathered crowd stood back, as if they expected more fighting.

"You took him out without killin' him."

"Is that a problem?"

"Hell, no. Big Willie's a good customer. I'd hate for him to leak whiskey if you ventilated him too many times." Allen laughed at his own joke.

"I have a beer waiting inside," Slocum said.

"Wait a minute. Let me buy you a real drink, Slocum. I got a proposition to make."

As they went inside, Allen chattered amiably, but Slocum noticed how none of the customers came over to speak to them. There had been gasps of astonishment when he had faced down Big Willie, then cheers when he had finally dispatched the cowboy. No one came close now that he was with Stanford Allen, and he wondered why.

"Morning, Mr. Allen," Morgan said, pulling up his torn shirt to hide his exposed union suit. "You want your regular?"

"Sure 'nuff, Morgan. And the same for my friend, John Slocum."

Slocum saw the flash of expression on Morgan's face. For a brief instant, there was contempt; then the barkeep turned impassive and scrounged under the bar for a bottle of Billy Taylor's finest.

"Brought a couple cases of this all the way from Kaintuck," Allen said proudly. "My own stock. Don't let just anyone drink it." He pushed a filled shot glass in Slocum's direction.

"How do I rate so high?"

"You're my new bouncer," Allen said. "Only the best for the man who keeps the peace in my saloons."

"I was moving on," Slocum said, sipping the whiskey.

For once, the label didn't lie. This was smooth liquor, about the best Slocum had sampled in a blue moon.

"You gotta stay. I'm hirin' you."

The way Allen spoke irritated Slocum. He assumed because he said it was so that it would happen. Still, when Slocum reflected on how empty his poke was, he knew a few silver dollars jingling in his pocket would get him a ways along the trail to wherever he was going.

"How much?" Slocum asked.

Allen studied him critically. The glint in his eye told how sure he was he had hooked Slocum.

"Dollar a day, room and board, and a shot of whiskey. Just one a day. More 'n that, you buy."

Slocum looked over at Morgan. The barkeep shook his head the barest amount.

"Two dollars a day," Slocum countered.

Allen spun and glared at his bartender. For a moment, Slocum thought the saloon owner was going to grab the barkeep around the throat and continue the throttling begun by Big Willie. Allen turned back. The dark fury burning on his face told Slocum he ought to be moving on.

Allen surprised him. Almost spitting it out, he said, "You're hired. Now get to work. I got this saloon and two others. You're responsible for keepin' the peace in all of 'em." With that, Stanford Allen swung around and stormed from the Crazy Eights.

Slocum stared at the swinging doors and wondered what he had gotten himself into. Morgan came over and slid a beer ahead of him.

"Fer you, Slocum. You're gonna need it, workin' for that son of a bitch."

"A mite testy," Slocum observed.

"More 'n that. He's got men gunnin' for him from here to Salt Lake City."

"He hired me as a bodyguard? I don't do that."

"It might come to that," Morgan said. "He owns the only

saloons in fifty miles and don't much care who he insults. Allen's got a fierce temper fer sich a puny fella."

Slocum worked on the beer and realized Morgan had been right earlier. The beer was bitter compared to the silky-smooth whiskey. Still, the price was right. Slocum worked on it until only foam remained. He wiped a spot off his lips, set down the mug with a loud click, and announced, "I'd better get to work. Where are the other saloons?"

He didn't need Morgan's directions to the other dives. The Castrated Bull was nothing more than a tent pitched at the outskirts of town. The few pasty-faced whores working there told Slocum this was likely to be moved around the county wherever there might be miners or other workers willing to spend their hard-earned money on whiskey and women. The people of Sage Junction avoided the Castrated Bull like the plague.

From the look of a couple of the soiled doves, plague wasn't too far from Slocum's mind either.

The third bar was a smaller version of the Crazy Eights. The Five Aces had been named after the poker hand Allen had used to win the deed, or so claimed one of the customers. The patron had left the saloon in a hurry, leaving most of his beer, when Allen had come in.

"You gettin' the feel of my properties, Slocum?" Allen demanded.

"You might double your take if you drank in private," Slocum said. "Just showing up causes your paying customers to leave."

"That's not funny." Allen's tone carried a razor's edge to it. "I don't hire men to insult me."

"The customers are afraid to do it to your face," Slocum said. "How'd you get such a reputation?"

"I made a big mistake hirin' you, Slocum. I—" Allen jerked around when the door crashed open. Big Willie Wilson filled the entrance, his broad shoulders brushing the doorjambs. Slocum almost laughed at the way the man's bowed legs formed an arch letting in the light from outside.

"You!" bellowed Big Willie. "I got a bone to pick with you!"

"Don't let him kill me," whined Allen. He moved to put Slocum between himself and the cowboy.

"Which of us are you talking to?" Slocum stood and pushed back his coat to free up his six-shooter.

"I don't much like you, Slocum," Big Willie said. "Not after you busted my goddamn nose and wrist. My dispute's with that big horse's ass."

"Slocum!" Allen grabbed Slocum's sleeve as he steered him around to stay between him and the mountain of gristle and meanness.

Slocum jerked free of Allen's feverish grip and stepped forward until he was only an inch from Big Willie.

"Buy you a drink," Slocum said.

"What?" Big Willie blinked. He was even uglier with a busted nose than he had been in his pristine condition. He squinted hard at Slocum. "You mean it?"

"I do," Slocum said. He heard Allen sputtering incoherently back in the saloon. He ignored his new boss. Working as a bouncer required more than a quick gun and a hard fist. Avoiding trouble or even making sure its causes were snuffed out mattered more.

"You're all right, Slocum," Big Willie said as Slocum stepped away to allow the cowboy into the saloon.

A signal to the weedy barkeep produced a bottle of whiskey and a pair of shot glasses.

"You're payin' fer this," Allen grumbled. He scuttled out of the saloon when both Slocum and Big Willie glared at him.

"I'll pay for it," Slocum told the barkeep. "Have Allen take it out of my day's wage."

He swapped drinks with Big Willie, sipping only a bit of the rotgut while the burly cowboy knocked back drink after drink and spilled his guts about his quarrel with Stanford

Allen. The gripe was mostly what Slocum had suspected. Allen was a muckworm and had cheated Big Willie in a business deal involving saddle horses and a couple cases of whiskey. By the time the cowboy was feeling no pain, Slocum went to the bar and told the barkeep, "He'll pass out if you give him a couple more drinks."

"You don't want that?"

Slocum shook his head at such stupidity.

"I want him snoring like he's sawing wood," Slocum said. "If he's passed out, he's not causing trouble. Where's Allen likely to be?"

The barkeep shrugged, then said, "Spends most all his time over at the Crazy Eights. Thinks that's a classier place than the Five Aces."

"Who'd have ever thought that?" Slocum before leaving took one last look at Big Willie to be sure he couldn't stand on his bandy legs. He had told Allen he wouldn't work as a personal bodyguard, and yet the saloon owner had intended for him to do just that. If he had been on a jury, Slocum would have decided in Big Willie's favor.

As he approached the Crazy Eights, he heard a ruckus inside. A chair sailed through the window and sloshed along a few feet in the muddy street. A slight man, hardly out of his teens, came staggering out, and barely caught himself before following the chair into the mud puddle.

"You can't do this!" he cried.

The young man fell to his knees when Allen roared out of the saloon and smashed a sawed-off shotgun barrel on the top of his head. Blood spattered and the man crumpled to his knees, holding his head. Allen swung the shotgun around like a baseball bat and hit him in the face. This propelled the man backward to land with a splash in the mud.

"You impudent son of a bitch. How dare ya say a thing like that to me? To *me*! Don't you know what I am? I'll larn you a lesson!"

Slocum moved fast when he saw the extent of Allen's lesson. The saloon owner lowered the shotgun and cocked both hammers. He intended to kill the young man struggling to sit up in the mud. From what Slocum could tell, the fallen man wasn't armed.

Arm sweeping upward, Slocum caught the barrels as Allen fired. Slocum winced as pain shot through his forearm where the suddenly hot metal barrels burned him.

"What are you doin', you stupid bastard? Your work fer me!" Allen fumbled to get two more shells from his coat pocket. Slocum squared off, swung, and knocked the man back through the window already broken by the chair.

"I don't work for the likes of you," Slocum said. Allen sputtered and struggled to get to his feet. He was wild-eyed and cut from glass shards.

"You're fired! You can't quit. I'm firin' you. *I'm* terminatin' yer employment! If I see you around my saloons again, I'll kill you, Slocum! I swear it!"

"Go to hell," Slocum said coldly. He turned his back on Allen and went to help the young man out of the mud, but he had already hightailed it. Slocum didn't blame him too much. Almost getting a double-barreled load of buckshot blasted into your belly could make a man skittish.

Slocum heard Allen thundering around inside the Crazy Eights. Morgan edged out and looked frightened.

"You git on outta here, Slocum. With him in a rage like that, there's no tellin' what he might do."

"I'm not inclined to let a pissant like him worry me none," Slocum said. "Thanks for the beers."

Slocum spun and walked away, knowing he would never get even a portion of the day's wages from Allen. Beating a dollar out of the man might be satisfying, but wasn't worth the effort. He had ridden into Sage Junction almost broke, and leaving without two nickels to rub together wasn't all that unusual for him. Once on the trail, he could bag a rabbit or two for dinner. Living off the land was easy enough in this mountainous country.

He went to the livery stable and found the owner.

"I'm moving on," he told the man.

"Not many stay in Sage Junction long," the liveryman allowed.

"Speaking of folks passing through, have you seen a woman in the past day or two?" Slocum described the dark-haired beauty he had seen talking to the Mormon girl and asking about the explosion back in the hills. The stable man shook his head.

"I'd remember any female what looked the way you said. All we got around here are plain-looking womenfolk."

"How about a young man?" Slocum didn't see any other animals being stabled. "He'd be all muddied up."

"Nope, nobody like that neither."

"Thanks," Slocum said, leading his horse from the stall. He saddled the mare, secured his tack, and then mounted. Riding from Sage Junction wasn't much different from leaving a hundred other towns. The only difference this time was that he'd left one man madder than a wet hen.

Slocum took what he thought was the road north, only to find it ended at a stream providing water for the town. He let his mare drink a bit, made sure his own canteen was full, then turned back toward Sage Junction to find the actual road. He remembered a town named Almy lay somewhere in that direction.

Twilight clutched at Sage Junction when he reached the main street. Slocum got his bearings and started his journey again, this time on what he was certain was the proper road north. Barely had he reached the last of the town's buildings when his mare reared. An instant later, the ground shook and an explosion from town sent fire and burning debris fountaining into the night sky.

He worked to keep his horse from bolting and turned toward Sage Junction. The fire blazed near the heart of town. Alarm bells summoned the volunteer fire department. Keeping the entire town from burning would be a backbreaking chore. Slocum trotted back to see what had happened.

He didn't have to ride far to see that the Crazy Eights saloon was the center of the raging fire. A charred barkeep splashed water on himself to put out the embers burning his clothing. Morgan looked up and pointed, his hand trembling.

"He did it. He killed Mr. Allen and set fire to the saloon!"

Slocum looked around to see who Morgan accused. He went cold when he realized he was the one being singled out as both arsonist and murderer.

3

Slocum sat and stared, not sure what was going on.

"Him, he did it," Morgan cried. The barkeep took a step, slipped in the mud, and fell to his knees, still pointing at Slocum.

A dozen men looked uncertainly from Slocum to Morgan and back.

"Your entire damn town's going to burn to the ground if you don't put out that fire," Slocum shouted. His deep voice cut through their confusion. The man wearing a fire captain's helmet began barking orders, and got his volunteers running around doing chores that forged them into a cohesive unit. Slocum watched a few minutes and backed away. His mare wanted to bolt from the fire, smoke, and bustle all around.

But when he turned the horse's head to ride on out, he found himself facing an old man holding a black powder Remington pistol in both hands. Even so, his aim was shaky and his eyes too rheumy for easy sighting. That didn't matter because Morgan stood behind him, a look of satisfaction on his soot-smeared face.

"That's him, Marshal. He's the one I told you about."

"Git on down from yer horse, Slocum," the marshal ordered. "Don't make me have to shoot. I ain't kilt a man in years and don't want to start again—but I will! I swear, I'll shoot if you make me!"

Slocum considered his chances and decided they were good. All he had to do was feint, get the old marshal to follow the movement, and he would be galloping from town too fast for anyone to track him. Most of the men were still working at fighting the fire. The Crazy Eights had gone up like a tinderbox and spewed sparks onto the buildings on either side. The one closest, a bakery, had burned, but the dry goods store on the other side had only smoldered a mite. The firemen had done a quick, efficient job once they got over their shock at actually seeing a fire in Sage Junction.

"Don't try makin' a break for it," said a loud voice behind Slocum. "I got you in my sights. I'll shoot if you try to run!"

Slocum glanced over his shoulder and saw it was worse than he expected. Not one, but three men had leveled their rifles at him. The marshal might miss. Hell, with the black powder pistol he waved around, he might blow off his own hand if he fired. Dodging bullets from three men behind him, though, was another matter.

"I don't know anything about the fire."

"He kilt Mr. Allen!" Morgan danced around and pointed his accusing finger at Slocum again. "My boss was in the Crazy Eights when it went up in flames. He must be dead from the fire and all."

"He is," someone called from the center of the burned-out saloon. "Ain't much left of him but that damned mustache of his and a lot of burned flesh and hair."

"You don't know it's Allen," Slocum said, playing for time. It hardly mattered whose body had been found. It would still be murder if the fire had been set.

"Why don't you jist step on down from that there animal?" the old geezer said, waving his ancient pistol around.

"His name's Slocum. He done it. He had a row with Mr. Allen and got fired."

"Don't go runnin' off at the mouth now, Morgan. I know his name. You shouted it at me 'nuff times. There's plenny of time fer testifying. Then we kin see about stringin' up this varmint."

Slocum considered how fast the men with rifles could react. He could beat the marshal if he drew and took a shot at Morgan. The barkeep deserved to have his tater trap shut permanently. Sounds of rifle hammers cocking stopped him.

"You're making a mistake," Slocum said. He kept his hands out where everyone could see that he wasn't going for his Colt Navy—as much as he wanted to. He swung his leg over the saddle horn and dropped with a splash into mud.

"Thass what they all say," the marshal declared. "I been marshal here for the last fifteen years and never once did I put a guilty man in the town lockup."

"I can believe that," Slocum said sarcastically. The words were lost on the townspeople. They pressed close to grab his six-shooter and search him for other weapons. When they took the knife he had sheathed in his boot, he realized how serious a fix he was in. He was a stranger to these people, and looked like a gunfighter on his way through town. It was easier for them to believe he had done the killing rather than one of their own.

He stared coldly at Morgan, who looked away guilty as sin.

"What happened?" Slocum asked. "I was out of town when I heard an explosion."

"Reckon you tossed a match into Mr. Allen's stock of alcohol in the back room. The whole damn place went up like you'd put dynamite under it."

Slocum frowned at Morgan's explanation. It didn't make a whole lot of sense. If it had happened the way the barkeep claimed, he would have gone up with Allen and the Crazy Eights Saloon. There was no way a man could outrun a blast like that.

"Git on down the street. The hoosegow's the fancy-ass building on the right," the marshal said.

"Don't you go lettin' him slip away like you did that rustler fellow last year," warned a man keeping his rifle aimed at Slocum's back.

"Marshal Pritchard's not gonna do that, Ben," said another. The two men got into a verbal fight over guarding Slocum. For a brief instant, Slocum thought he might use the argument to his advantage; then he saw Morgan with a six-gun of his own. The barkeep was waiting for Slocum to make a break so he could gun him down.

This set Slocum's mind to working on other ways of getting away. However that might be, it had to happen after the men with the rifles went back to their chores. And Morgan wasn't going to stand guard all night waiting for Slocum to escape. Having a section of the town burned down meant more work for everyone.

"You the new owner of the Crazy Eights?" Slocum asked Morgan.

"Why, uh, I ain't thought on it. Things happened too quick."

"Sure, you're the new owner," Marshal Pritchard said to Morgan. "Who else'd want it? All you got's a pile of burned lumber, but it kin be the best waterin' hole in Sage Junction again with a little work."

"What about the other two places?"

"What's the interest you got in all this, Slocum?" Pritchard asked.

"Just considering who might really want to kill Allen. The men who'd profit usually deserve to be considered suspects in any murder."

"Well, now, I ain't—"

"Don't listen to him, Marshal," Morgan said loudly. "He's tryin' to worm outta hangin'."

"Might have been an accident, too," said Slocum. "Like Morgan said, that back room was filled with whiskey and alcohol. A spark could have set it off. Who's most likely to do that but the owner?"

"He's tryin' to confuse you," Morgan said. "You don't let him—"

"You kin get mighty tiresome, son," Marshal Pritchard said to Morgan. "You go do what you have to do. I'll tend to *my* prisoner."

Pritchard herded Slocum into the jailhouse. From the outside, it looked as decrepit as the marshal. Slocum's heart sank when he saw the iron cage at the rear of the single room. Two-inch-wide iron straps formed the sides and top and, from what he could tell, went under the dirt floor. This wasn't a cell as much as it was a complete cage.

"Yup, you figgered it out, Slocum. Ain't nobody's ever got out of my jailhouse. Not 'less they was supposed to go. Git yer ass on into the cell now, you hear?"

The door clanged shut. Slocum turned and watched as Pritchard locked the hefty padlock. A chain had been run around two of the iron straps, and it fastened the door shut with the biggest lock Slocum had ever seen. Pritchard tossed the key into the air and snared it with surprising dexterity.

"You gotta git up mighty early in the mornin' to escape outta my jail," the old marshal said, shuffling to a desk situated as far from the cell as possible. He tucked the key into the center drawer, then locked it with a smaller key and made a big show of dangling that smaller key from a string around his neck.

Slocum turned from thinking of ways to get the padlock key to examining the cell. It took only a few minutes before he realized he wasn't getting out of jail anytime soon.

"When's the trial?" Slocum called to the marshal. Pritchard had hiked his feet on to the desktop and leaned back. His head snapped up as he fought sleep. He had almost been asleep.

"Trial? We got a circuit judge comin' on through in a week or so. Jist be glad we're in Wyoming and not Utah.

They got ferocious judges across the territorial boundary, they do. Judge McAfee's honest enough and fair."

"You have many hangings in Sage Junction?"

"Only the ones the judge approves of."

"That means a fair number."

"Ain't been six months since the last. The gallows we built all special rotted away, but we kin throw up another. Or find a sturdy tree limb."

"I want to look over the Crazy Eights."

"What fer? You done burnt it to the ground with Stanford Allen inside."

"I need to find evidence to prove I didn't do it," Slocum said. Anything that got him out of this cell increased his chances for escape. Having a new wanted poster dogging his heels didn't bother him too much. He was already wanted for a dozen different crimes, the worst being for killing a federal judge.

After the war, he had returned to the family farm in Georgia intending to heal up both physically and emotionally. His parents were dead and his brother Robert had been cut down during Pickett's Charge. Raising crops on the farm that had been in the Slocum family since it had been deeded over by King George I was all he had wanted, but a carpetbagger judge had other ideas.

No taxes paid. The land was forfeit. Clear out now. That's what the judge had decreed, and he had ridden out with a hired gunman to enforce his own order. Slocum had followed the letter of the law when it came to vacating the premises. He had also ridden off after leaving two filled graves down near the springhouse. Killing a judge, even a federal judge, was a serious crime.

If Judge McAfee caught wind of that crime, there was no way in hell Slocum would walk away a free man. He snorted as he considered the facts. This was a hostile town, and not one likely to value the truth highly if it meant one of their own had committed the crime. Better to ignore what Morgan might have done and cleanse their conscience by lynching a stranger. More than this, Slocum doubted too many in Sage Junction were going to shed a tear over Allen's death.

Marshal Pritchard began snoring so loud Slocum wanted to smother him. He ran the links of the chain holding the cell door shut through his hands, hunting for any weakness. Like the broad straps surrounding him on all sides, the chain and lock were secure. He finally collapsed on the hard cot, thinking hard. Escaping was not likely to happen.

He looked up when the outer door creaked open. His heart leaped in his chest when he saw Big Willie Wilson poke his battered face inside. Big Willie put his finger to his lips to keep Slocum silent.

The cowboy made his way to the cell and looked at Slocum curiously.

"You come to get me out?" Slocum asked, but he hardly believed this was going to happen. He had battered the cowboy's face and humiliated him. There was no reason to free the man who did that—and, Slocum had to admit, Big Willie could well be the murderer. He hated Allen more than anyone else Slocum knew in town. Having another man blamed for the crime would suit Big Willie just fine, if he were the killer and arsonist.

"Naw, I came to see if what I heard was true. You really killed that mangy cayuse? I gotta hand it to you, Slocum. You done us all a favor."

"I didn't kill Allen," Slocum said, trying to keep his voice down. As long as Big Willie didn't wake the marshal, there was a ghost of a chance the cowboy might spring him.

"Who else'd do it?"

"I was on my way out of town when the Crazy Eights blew up. I wasn't anywhere near it." Slocum frowned. Something about what he just said caused a thought to bubble up in his brain, but he couldn't figure out why it was important.

"Settin' fire to a couple feet o' miner's fuse ain't so hard," Big Willie said thoughtfully. "Hell, even I kin do that."

"Why would I come back if I'd done that?"

Slocum saw that reason wasn't going to work with Big Willie.

"Why did you come by?" Slocum asked.

"Well," the cowboy said slowly, "I suppose it was to be sure you're actually here and alive." He pressed his fingers into his shirt pocket. Slocum saw the outline of a tiny coin.

"That a twenty-dollar gold piece? In your pocket?" Slocum asked.

Big Willie jerked his hand away as if he had burned it on a stove. "Why'd you ask that?"

"You didn't have any money over at the Five Aces. I bought you a drink," Slocum reminded him. "You owe me."

"You busted my goddamn nose."

"You were bullying Morgan," Slocum said.

"That sure worked out real good for you, didn't it? Might be you should have let me rough him up. He's as big a son of a bitch as Allen."

"He killed his boss and set fire to the Crazy Eights. I know he did it," Slocum said. "Get me out of here, and I'll prove it."

Big Willie sucked on his gums for a few seconds, then shook his head.

"No way am I bustin' you outta here," the cowboy said. "I was jist supposed to . . ."

"You were supposed to do what, Big Willie?" Slocum perked up at the way the cowboy spoke. "Who paid you to come check on me?"

"I cain't tell you that, Slocum. I promised."

"That *is* a twenty-dollar gold piece in your shirt pocket. Who paid you twenty dollars to come in here?"

Marshal Pritchard snorted, and one foot fell off the desk to crash into the floor. The lawman jerked around, grumbled, and rubbed at his eyes. He didn't see so good at the best of times. Slocum knew that from the way the marshal had aimed his Remington out in the street, but he didn't have to have perfect eyesight to see Big Willie Wilson in his jail-house.

"Get me out of here!" Slocum said urgently. He tried to reach out and pull in Big Willie, but the cowboy stepped back far enough so Slocum's grabbing hand missed by inches.

"I don't wanna get in dutch with the law," Big Willie said. "Allen cheated me, and the marshal wouldn't do nuthin'. Nobody in this damned town crossed Allen without payin' fer it."

"If you think I killed Allen, set me free!"

Big Willie stared at the marshal. Pritchard snorted again and rubbed his nose. He sneezed hard enough to cause his other foot to slip from the desk. The marshal fumbled around in his pocket and pulled out a filthy handkerchief to wipe his nose.

The cowboy edged toward the door, slipped through, and disappeared into the night. Slocum sagged against the iron straps. He cursed under his breath. He had been close to getting Big Willie to open the door. He knew it. Somebody had paid the bowlegged cowboy to be sure he was locked up.

For the life of him, Slocum couldn't figure out who that might be. Morgan need only poke his ugly face in to talk to the marshal about his prisoner. Nobody else Slocum knew in town had any call to give Big Willie a plugged nickel since they could drop in, too.

A wild thought straightened Slocum. If Stanford Allen was still alive and pulling some kind of swindle, he couldn't allow himself to be seen. If he wanted to know that Slocum was securely locked up, he might pay off Big Willie. Even as the notion blossomed, it wilted. Allen would never hire Big Willie—and Big Willie could never have completed his mission without spilling his guts. He believed Allen was dead. Slocum doubted Big Willie was good enough an actor to convince anyone of a lie.

Slocum dropped back onto his cot. The only thing he had to work with was a wood leg from the cot. He doubted he could pick the lock with a splinter, but using the leg when Marshal Pritchard decided to feed him was probably his only hope, faint as it was. Dropping to the floor, he began tugging on the leg to get it free. Propping the cot against the wall would keep it from being obvious that it was missing a leg. He couldn't lie on it without falling, but—

"What are you doing?"

Slocum spun around, the dirt floor tearing at his knees. He thought the marshal had caught him. Then a million small things told him this wasn't the marshal.

He looked at a gingham dress and worked up past the trim waist and pert breasts to the pale oval face framed in raven-wing-dark hair. Eyes so blue it almost hurt peered at him.

"Trying like hell to get out of here," he said.

"That won't work," the young woman told him softly. "This iron is too hard, and the lock and chain are quite expensive. For a small town like Sage Junction, it is impressive that so much was spent on the lockup."

"What will work to get me out?"

The question amused her. A smile curled the corners of her ruby lips, and Slocum thought she was going to laugh out loud.

"Why, all you have to do is ask."

Slocum asked.

4

The woman ran her fingers over the padlock, much as Slocum had done earlier. She softly rested it against the iron cage, then turned and went to the sleeping marshal. Pritchard snorted and stirred in his desk chair, but the woman never slowed as she went to him as silent as a ghost. He sniffed and rubbed his nose with his sleeve before settling back in his chair.

"There's a string around his neck with the key to his desk drawer," Slocum said. His words caused Pritchard to stir and mumble something incoherent.

The woman held up her hand to silence Slocum. She turned slightly and mouthed, "I know." With the touch of a surgeon, she pulled back the marshal's grimy collar and flicked at the string with her fingernail. When she teased a loop upward, she caught it and began drawing it out of the man's shirt.

Slocum watched in silence. His heart hammered loud enough to awaken the lawman, but Pritchard slept on as the woman slipped the string off his neck and held up the desk key as if she had just landed an eight-pound trout. Sliding her thumb and index finger down the string, she snared the key. In less than one of Slocum's fierce heartbeats, she had the desk drawer open and the padlock key removed.

"Here," she said, handing him that key. For a moment, their hands touched. She did not recoil as Slocum had almost expected her to do. If anything, there was a special gleam in her eye. Whether it was one of superiority at getting him out of a jam he was trapped in, or something more, Slocum decided he could find out later. Either one was fine with him.

The key slid into the lock and made a metallic click as it opened the cell door for him. He spun out, but the woman held up her hand again and put her finger to her lips, cautioning him to silence. She plucked the padlock key from him, went back to the desk, and returned it to the drawer. Swiftly locking the desk drawer, she gingerly returned the string holding the small key to the marshal's neck. He stirred again and swatted at his neck, as if an insect had bitten him.

While she did all this, Slocum strapped on his gun belt, slipped his six-shooter into the holster, and returned his knife to its boot sheath. If the marshal awoke now, he would face an escaping prisoner armed to the teeth.

Walking softly, the woman went to the door, peered out into the night, and then signaled Slocum to follow. He slid through the small space between door and frame, and held down the impulse to howl at the setting moon like some lovelorn coyote. It felt damned good to be free again.

"Your horse is around back," she said.

They faced each. Slocum saw she was taller than he had first thought. He stood an even six feet, and she was only three or four inches shorter. That made her just the right height for kissing. He bent slightly and planted a big kiss on her lips. She stepped back and looked startled as her hand rose to her mouth.

"Thanks," he said. "I don't know why you got me out of there, but I appreciate it."

"Then don't get caught," she said. "The marshal is an old man, but he's not senile. Rumor has it he was once the best tracker in western Wyoming. There might be some skill remaining."

"I'll cover my tracks," Slocum said. He hesitated, then asked, "Why'd you get me out?"

"Justice," she said cryptically. She pushed him away and dashed off into the dark. From what Slocum could tell of the stars above, it was about five or six hours until dawn. He had to make the best of the time if he wanted to get clear of Sage Junction.

Circling the building brought him to where his mare had been tethered. He vaulted into the saddle and headed out of town. Before, he had ridden north. Whether any of the townspeople knew that or not, he chose another direction at random. West into Utah allowed him to travel faster since the mountains were flattening out into rocky plains.

Barely had he ridden a mile when he heard hoofbeats on the road behind him. He cursed under his breath. The only rider at this time of night had to be the marshal coming after him for busting out of jail. Slocum rode off the trail and hunted for a spot to hole up until he could see if Marshal Pritchard had recruited a posse that he couldn't hear yet. It was inconceivable that the old lawman would ride after an escaped prisoner alone.

A wooded area not twenty yards off the road gave some cover and let him watch the stretch of road leading toward town. Slocum drew his six-shooter and checked the cylinder to be sure he carried a full load. He normally rode with the hammer resting on an empty chamber, but not now. He wanted to be able to fling as much lead as possible, if it came to a gunfight.

The galloping horse approached. Slocum craned his neck and peered through the low-hanging branch of a mountain maple tree. The pistol lifted when pale starlight flashed off the bridle of the rider out on the trail. He lowered it when he saw only the solitary horseman. No posse.

And this wasn't Marshal Pritchard.

His lovely benefactor galloped past and kept going down

the road. Slocum returned his six-shooter to its holster and then urged his mare back to the road. The sound of hoof-beats ahead lured him on. The woman had rescued him and had demanded nothing in return. She said she had let him out of the cell because of justice, and Slocum wanted to know what she meant by that. In all his travels, the justice most likely to prevail came from the business end of a six-gun or at the end of a rope.

He trotted after her, knowing her breakneck speed wasn't possible to maintain for more than a mile or two. The stars cast silver-bright light on the road, giving him a decent view of the hoofprints in the road. Long after he ceased hearing the pounding hooves of the flying horse ahead, he kept riding. A slow smile came to his lips when he saw the tracks leading off the road. She had ridden the horse to exhaustion and had to rest now.

The tracks crossed a grassy spot and went into a stand of trees some distance from the road. Slocum turned wary as he got closer. He had the feeling of being watched. This sixth sense had served him well during and after the war. Taking off his hat, he waved it slowly in the air to attract attention. If somebody watched him, this was showing he meant no harm. If nobody watched, Slocum could feel stupid and also glad that no one else knew how edgy he was following a young woman so intent on running.

He put his hat back on and advanced. Slocum was glad that he had been so cautious. The woman stepped from behind a tree, a rifle to her shoulder.

"Why'd you follow me?" she called.

"Was the other way around. I lit out on the road, heard you coming fast, and decided to see who was out so late."

She lowered the rifle. Starlight caught her eyes and turned them into liquid silver. Slocum rode closer, but did not dismount.

"I had a question," Slocum said.

"You're a mighty curious fellow to risk so much."

Slocum shook his head. He doubted there was much

risk. She might be a decent shot with the rifle, but hitting a mounted rider in the dark took a damned fine marksman.

"So what's the question?" A note of irritation had entered her words. Slocum reckoned she was waiting for someone and wanted to get rid of unwanted visitors, namely John Slocum.

"What's your interest in the explosion up in the hills a couple days back?"

The woman lifted the rifle to her shoulder again, but it was from a shocked reaction. She never trained it on him, but could lift and fire in an instant.

"That's the strangest question I've ever been asked."

"So?"

"What makes you think I'm interested in any old explosion?"

"You gave Lenore a piece of peppermint candy."

"This conversation is the strangest I've ever had. Who's Lenore?"

"The Mormon girl with the settlers. You asked her about the blast."

"I'm just like you, Mr. Slocum. I'm naturally curious about what's going on around me. The explosion occurred as I rode through the mountain pass and I wondered what had happened."

Slocum appreciated how easily and well she lied—but she'd told a whopper.

"What caused the blast? There weren't any railroaders or miners blasting for pay dirt in the area."

"The only mining is a ways down the road in the foothills of the Wasatch Mountains," she said.

"Mind if I dismount? My horse doesn't mind me riding her all night long, but standing gets to be a chore."

The woman laughed and lowered the rifle again, saying, "I can appreciate both sentiments."

"Both?" Slocum's eyebrows arched. It took a lot to surprise him, but this lovely woman managed to do so repeatedly.

"Standing overlong hurts my knees," she said. When she turned and walked away from him, he barely heard, "And I love being ridden all night."

Slocum followed her through the trees to where she had left her horse. There hadn't been time for her to make a proper camp, but she had obviously intended to stay here a spell. She had unsaddled her horse and scattered out preparations for a meal.

"If you're cooking, mind if I join you?" he asked.

"Mr. Slocum, I got you free from that awful jail because you did not belong there. Do not confuse an act of charity for anything more."

Her words said one thing, but Slocum saw the set to her body, the way she thrust out her chest just a little more than usual and stood with one hand on a cocked hip. He sank down to a fallen log and looked up at her.

"Why didn't you think Marshal Pritchard had the right man?"

"I—you—I saw you riding in as the saloon erupted in flames." She fumbled with her words and some of her cocksure attitude faded. It came back in a rush. "I heard what was said about the fire. It was obvious to any fool that you could not have been responsible."

"I'm glad there was one fool in Sage Junction willing to believe that."

"You're calling me a fool?" She flushed and the hand on her hip turned into a tight fist.

"I have to call you something since I don't know your name. Nobody in town knew it either."

"You asked around?" This flustered her even more.

"Not everybody is generous enough to give a Mormon girl a peppermint candy," he said.

"Sarah Beth."

"Her name was Lenore," Slocum said before he realized he had just been given his benefactor's name.

She moved closer, her skirt whispering as she moved. A

small breeze blew, but the movement of her gingham came from long, shapely legs beneath the skirt. Slocum knew that because Sarah Beth hiked up her skirt as she came to straddle his waist. She settled down, her crotch pushed up close to his. Their faces were only inches apart. Slocum was surprised again to find he had been wrong about her.

Sarah Beth was not beautiful. She was gorgeous.

This time she kissed him. She threw her arms around his neck and pulled him closer so their lips first brushed lightly and then crushed together in mounting passion. Slocum held her tightly and let his hands rove up and down her back, tracing out every bone in her spine. She began rubbing back and forth, moving on his lap. She broke off the kiss and said, "Your gun belt."

Slocum replied, "Your dress."

Each knew what the other meant. Something had to go. Slocum rocked back and unfastened his gun belt and dropped it on the ground. Sarah Beth grabbed the hem of her skirt and lifted it out of the way. She remained standing as Slocum worked down the row of buttons on his fly. He let out a gasp of relief when his erection popped free, and Sarah Beth caught her breath.

"So nice," she said, settling back down over his legs. Slocum felt his hardness rubbing against already damp nether lips. She wiggled around a little, then lifted and positioned herself properly to slowly lower around him.

He sank into her hot core and was quickly surrounded by gripping tightness. She moaned softly as she leaned backward and ground herself down into his lap. Slocum braced himself on the log and simply sat for a moment, willing himself not to act like a young buck with his first woman.

Everything was as perfect as possible. A woman heartachingly beautiful and all the time in the world. He gripped her around the waist and began moving her up and down in a rhythm that set both their pulses to racing.

Slocum bent forward and kissed Sarah Beth's throat and

then worked lower. He plucked at buttons on her dress, and opened a deep vee that exposed the tops of her breasts. He licked and kissed over the tender surfaces, until she reached up and yanked hard, ripping cloth and fully exposing them to his lips.

He caught one rosebud nipple and sucked hard. Sarah Beth let out a groan of pure delight. He pressed his tongue into it and then raked it with his teeth. Then he pulled back and blew. The combination of his saliva and the cooling breath caused her to jerk.

"Oh, I've never felt that before," she sighed. "Hot, cold, hard, wet, it's setting me on fire all over."

"I know," Slocum said. He had felt her tightening around him, making him feel as if he had thrust himself into a tight velvet glove. When she twisted from side to side, it gave him sensations he had yearned for over the last few weeks. The trail had been long from Denver. He had appreciated being alone, but knew now he needed female companionship to bring his senses completely alive.

He returned to the deep valley between her snowy breasts. He licked and kissed his way to the coral-capped tip, and then slid back down and up the other tip to give it similar attention. All the while, he held her tightly.

He found guiding her was easier if he cupped her firm buttocks. The play of muscle as she rose and dropped on his hardness thrilled him almost as much as the feel of her all around him.

"I knew there was a reason I got you out," Sarah Beth said hotly in his ear before nibbling on it. Her tongue lashed out and danced about, giving Slocum even more stimulation.

"I'm glad you're curious," Slocum said.

"Curious?"

"About explosions."

She tensed and tried to push away. He wouldn't let her. He gazed into her eyes and saw his words had robbed some of the sexual thrill from her.

"You wanted to see an explosion," Slocum said. "The

way you excite me, you're going to be on the receiving end of one any instant."

The tension evaporated and Sarah Beth laughed in delight. Then she gasped as she began working up and down faster. Friction mounted, and each was lost in a wonderland of delicious sensation. As Slocum had predicted, an explosion was close at hand. He felt the heat bubbling deep in his balls, and no matter how he tried to hold back to prolong the lovemaking, it inexorably moved upward until he cried out in release.

His cries were matched by Sarah Beth's. They clung to each other, hips grinding as they thrashed about. Slocum was aware of losing his balance. He pulled the woman hard to his body as they tumbled to the ground. Still locked together, they rolled over and over and finally came to rest, her knees up on either side of his body while he propped himself up on his hands. He looked down into her eyes.

They were now glazed with the afterglow of good sex.

Slocum reflected on how much had changed in his life over the past few days. He had befriended settlers, endured an explosion, was on the run from the law for a murder he didn't commit, and had just made love to the gorgeous woman who had rescued him from jail.

"Why are you interested in the blast up in the hills?" he asked.

Sarah Beth tensed and then visibly forced herself to relax, and snuggled closer in the circle of his arms.

"I'm just a curious person. Don't you wonder what caused the explosion?"

"Not to the extent of seeking out a settler's kid to ask about it," Slocum said.

"I don't deal well with adults," Sarah Beth said.

"That's not true," Slocum said. "You dealt well a few minutes ago. I'd call it a royal flush."

"Dealing? That's what you call it? I call it . . ."

She showed him what she meant. This time, after they finished, Slocum leaned against the fallen log and nodded off. When he awoke from his nap an hour later, Sarah Beth was gone. He considered tracking her, then decided he ought to hightail it as far from Sage Junction as possible. For once in his life, he could ignore a mystery.

Even one as beguiling as Sarah Beth.

5

Slocum cursed as he switched shoulders, moving the heavy saddle and almost dropping his saddlebags. His horse had stepped in a gopher hole two miles back, and he'd had to shoot her. On foot, he had spent more time looking over his shoulder for a posse on his trail than he did looking ahead. From a weather-beaten sign along the trail, he knew he wasn't far from the town of Border, perched on the boundary between Wyoming and Utah.

The rattle of a buckboard coming from higher up in the mountains to his right caused Slocum to drop his saddle and take a break. He watched as the driver slowed and gave him a once-over, then pulled hard on the reins to stop.

"Howdy," Slocum called.

"Howdy," the driver replied. "You lookin' fer a lift into town?"

"That'd be mighty neighborly of you." Slocum explained about his horse's fate. "Damned good horse. Sorry to see her go down with a busted leg like that."

"Hard to find reliable nags out here." The driver snapped the reins and a long-eared mule brayed. "I prefer these beasties. Nasty-tempered, but they can pull all day."

"You going into town for supplies?"

"Am." The driver looked hard at Slocum, pointed to the empty buckboard, and waited for saddle and gear to be tossed in. Slocum climbed up beside the driver.

"Name's Micah Snell," the driver said. After Slocum introduced himself, Snell said, "You got the look of a man down on his luck."

"I was doing fine until a broken leg changed all that," Slocum lied. He forced himself not to look back to see if Marshal Pritchard had a posse after him. There had been no sign of pursuit, but the biblical aphorism about the wicked fleeing when no man pursued kept coming to mind.

"You wantin' a job?"

"I can use a dollar or two and would swap a day's work for it."

"I can't get enough miners," Snell said. "I'm the headman up at the Shady Lady Mine. Not the best claim I ever had, but it's makin' money."

"That's more than I can say," Slocum admitted.

"You ever work in a mine? Or are you only a cowboy lookin' for cattle to herd?"

"There any kind of ranching around here?"

"Not so much. A few small spreads. A bit more farming, but the ground's mighty rocky. Most all are family operations. Mormons tend to extended families, too, so hirin' outsiders ain't somethin' that's done overmuch."

"Anything available in town?" Slocum asked.

Snell laughed at this, but didn't say anything more. Slocum found out why. Border was a small town with an "us against them" attitude. The owner of the general store was barely civil to Snell, and wouldn't even speak to Slocum as he helped load flour and beans into the buckboard. By the time they were rattling out of town, heading into the mountains toward the Shady Lady Mine, Slocum was resigned to working a spell buried under a mountain of rock.

He needed the money to buy another horse, but the job

presented a danger, more than working underground scrabbling for specks of gold. If Marshal Pritchard came looking, Slocum would be easy to find. He had to blend in quickly with the other miners so nobody asking after him would give him a second glance. The possibility that he hoped for, but could not count on, was the old lawman giving up on finding his arson and murder suspect. How badly the marshal had been stung by having his prisoner spirited away under his nose would have a lot to do with his determination in bringing Slocum to justice.

Or what passed for it in Sage Junction.

"You're mighty quiet, Slocum." Snell snapped the reins and got the mule team pulling hard to get up a steep hill.

"Not much to say."

"You won't fit in with my miners. They're a bunch of chatterin' magpies. Never seen a lot of men who go on like they do. Don't much care as long as they bring out the ore."

The mules gasped and wheezed, and finally pulled over the rise and onto a flat leading over to the Shady Lady Mine. Slocum's eyes widened in surprise. He had expected a small operation. Four mine shafts plunged into the mountainside and each showed tailings spewing forth. A small town housed the bunkhouse, mess hall, and several other buildings. One building caught Slocum's eye right away.

"That there's where we store the gold 'fore shippin' it over to Salt Lake City," Snell said. "Harder to get into than any bank vault, if that's any interest to you."

"You're pulling that much out of the mine?"

"The Shady Lady is a real purty lady. She's as close to bein' my sweetheart as I'm likely to find," Snell said, drawing to a halt by the mess hall. "Go on and unload. I'll wrangle up the mine foreman to show you what needs doing."

Slocum looked around. Twilight cast long shadows everywhere, but the miners were nowhere to be seen.

"We work twenty hours a day, ten hours each on two shifts," said a raspy voice. "Mr. Snell said you're the new mucker."

"And beast of burden," Slocum said, getting a sack of flour to his shoulder.

"You won't be treated near as good," the man said. "I'm Windsor. My friends call me Lucky, but don't bother. You ain't my friend and you never will be."

"Nice to know," Slocum said, kicking open the door into the mess hall. He found the pantry and settled the heavy bag of flour, then made several more trips to empty the rest of the supplies from the wagon. Windsor made no effort to help. Slocum had the feeling of being watched like a snake watches a bird.

"Git yer gear to the bunkhouse. You got a half hour 'fore the next shift goes into the mine. You'll work it till I say different."

"You work that shift?"

"Naw, I work the day shift so I can sleep at night like a real human bein'," Windsor said. "You ain't in that category, so don't get any ideas. You ever muck a mine?"

Slocum nodded. He swung his saddle and saddlebags around and headed for the bunkhouse, Windsor peppering him with questions the entire distance. Slocum answered the best he could.

"You ever do any blastin'?"

"Some," Slocum said. He found an empty bunk and stowed his gear under it. From the number of beds already claimed, more than thirty men worked the mines. "Where's the rest of my shift?"

"We're blastin' tonight. They're over at the storage shed bein' told what to do—and what not to do. Wouldn't want any of 'em gettin' their damn fool heads blowed off."

"Nope, wouldn't like that. Any chance I can grab some food?"

"Get on over to the shed," Windsor said. "You eat with your shift and they were done a half hour back."

Slocum's belly growled, but he knew better than to argue the point. He stowed his six-shooter and folded his duster to use as a pillow later. After the day he'd already had, finishing his shift in ten hours would leave him dog tired.

Not that he hadn't gotten some sleep after his tryst with Sarah Beth. For a brief moment, he wondered where she had gone—and who she had ridden out of Sage Junction to meet. An arrow fired at a target couldn't have been more into the bull's-eye than the lovely woman heading for the spot where Slocum had found her. Whoever she'd met was a mighty lucky fellow.

Slocum passed the gold storage building, and saw what Snell meant about this being more secure than a bank vault. The walls were thick and the door was heavy metal secured with three heavy padlocks. He shook his head. It must be something in the water in these parts. Sage Junction's jail was about as tight as any he had ever seen. And Snell had undoubtedly made sure no mole would dig up into his vault or bird peck down through the roof. Most of all, nobody was getting through the door into that vault who wasn't invited.

The thought of actually lightening Snell's burden of so much gold faded. Slocum liked the man, and saw nothing wrong doing an honest day's work for a decent wage. In a month or so, he would have enough to buy a broke-down horse and be on his way. If the miners were poor poker players, he might cut that time to a couple weeks. After all, what else was there to do miles from a town that didn't cotton much to strangers? Try as he might, Slocum couldn't remember seeing a saloon in Border.

"Git yer ass over here," growled a man almost as thick through the chest as he was tall. If he topped five-foot-five, it would have surprised Slocum. The man looked to have been born ready for the mines: short, powerful, with a brawler's battered face and hands the size of cured Virginia hams.

"I'm the shift foreman." He glared at Slocum, dark eyes boring into Slocum's green ones. Slocum did not flinch. The foreman finally broke off the staring contest. "I'm Seamus Rourke, and I don't bloody care who you are. You ever see the like of this before?" Rourke held up a spool of waxy black miner's fuse.

Slocum nodded.

"Then you know how to set it and how fast she burns. We got a whale of a lot of rock to bring down for the day shift. Mr. Snell's found a new vein. It's up to us to expose it for those worthless clinkers to bring out and get all the credit. We split into teams. You're with me." Rourke poked his finger into Slocum's chest.

Slocum resisted the urge to break the man's finger, then work up to his bull neck. Something in the effort it took to keep from tearing the man apart communicated to the night foreman. Rourke backed off.

"On second thought, you and Rick are a team. I'll go with Hastings. Drill in three feet, load the bore, and draw out the fuse. We'll light together so nobody's in the mine. Git yer gear and let's do some work, for a change."

"Rick," said a slight balding man with an X scar on his cheek. He thrust out his hand. Slocum shook. For all the fragility in the man's frame, his grip was strong and his hand calloused from hard work in the mine.

Slocum introduced himself, then said, "Is he always so disagreeable?"

"Don't think bad about Shameless." Seeing Slocum's expression, Rick laughed and said, "Shameless Seamus, that's what we call 'im, but not to 'is face. The other side of being so venomous is that he don't know shit about mining. He looks tough and talks like 'e knows, but I swear, 'e'll get us all killed with the way 'e blasts."

"You a powder man?"

"I hail from Bucks County. Third-generation coal miner until union trouble. I moved out West and found gold mining more profitable."

"Not as much coal dust to suck into your lungs either," Slocum said, wrestling a case of dynamite and a spool of black miner's fuse into the mine shaft.

"You know the business then," Rick said. He lit a carbide

lamp and put it on a strap, settling it around his head. Then he started another for Slocum. "I'll fit it. Don't go droppin' the dynamite. Ain't the best quality, bein' old, and it might go off."

Slocum shifted his head from side to side and got the miner's lamp settled down comfortably. He now was able to make out the well-worn tracks leading deeper into the mine. Where the ore cart was he didn't know, since he hadn't seen one outside this shaft.

"We got a ways to hike. Watch your head. You're a tall one for this kind of work."

Rick yammered away as they made their way deeper into the mine. Slocum was reminded of what Snell had said about the miners being a talkative lot. Not paying a lot of attention, Slocum began examining the layers of rock in the mine. In more than one place, he caught the glint of gold. From the strata, it might be fool's gold, but in other places where the drifts angled away to follow a vein of ore, he knew that a considerable amount of gold had been pulled from the rock already.

"Snell owns all this?"

"That's what we all think," Rick said. "Never 'eard of a partner, but there could be one, maybe in Salt Lake City. 'E's a nice old fella, but 'e's got a knack of hirin' sons of bitches to work for 'im." Rick stopped and turned, looking sheepish. Slocum's eye-searing purple carbide light caused the X scar on his cheek to shine. "Didn't mean you, Slocum. Hell, don't know you."

"I've met Windsor, and Shameless Seamus Rourke is a piece of work."

Rick laughed. "You're gonna fit right in. Most of the other miners are all right, if you don't get them too drunk or say somethin' they don't like."

"How much gold comes out of this mine?"

"Don't know since there's so many tunnels and two shifts of us chippin' away all the time, but I've heard tell of eight ounces to the ton."

Slocum let out a low whistle.

"No wonder that building is like a fortress," he said.

"Where Mr. Snell stores the gold? Yeah, it's a fort," Rick said. "No way of stealin' from it. If you're thinkin' on it—and I don't advise it—snarin' a load as it comes from the smelter in the next canyon over's the way to do it."

Slocum shook his head and said, "I'll be content to make a few dollars before moving on. It wouldn't be so bad if Snell paid in gold."

Rick laughed harshly.

"Ain't never gonna 'appen. 'E loves 'is precious gold. Always pays in scrip issued on a Salt Lake City bank. 'Ere we are. You want to hold the bit?" Rick looked at him expectantly.

Holding the bit required less skill and a lot of trust that the man swinging the ten-pound hammer didn't miss. There wasn't a great deal of room to dodge if a swing went wild or slipped off the metal tip after a poorly aimed blow.

"You've had more practice, I reckon," Slocum said. He hefted a five-foot-long steel bit. From the brightness of the tip, it had been sharpened recently.

Rick heaved a sigh of relief, but said nothing as he picked up the hammer and waited to see where Slocum placed the bit. Slocum was in no hurry. Getting a hole started took some judgment. He pressed his face close to the rock wall and brushed off dust and pulled at loose pebbles until he found a suitable spot.

"'Ow come you didn't go with the cracked spot? It's easier to drive a 'ole there."

Slocum rotated the bit to start a small pit in the rock, then shifted his grip on the shaft back a couple feet.

"You don't want to blast along a crack. There's no telling what might happen when the dynamite goes off."

Rick smiled and began swinging.

"We're gonna make a fine team, Slocum. You got brains, and I got muscle." Rick swung powerfully and began the arduous task of drilling into the hard rock.

Sweating and tired, Slocum finally pulled out the drill bit after a half hour of hammering, and tossed it to the floor with a loud clank. Dust from the drilling had risen and made his eyes water. He held back a sneeze as he blew hard on the hole to clear it of the fine dust. A quick twist of his head shone the light of the lamp deep into the hole and all around. He looked over his shoulder at Rick and nodded.

"We've got it," he said.

"You know 'ow to stuff in the explosive?"

Slocum worked to open the crate with the four sticks of dynamite resting in a bed of excelsior. He slid them into the hole one by one until the final one stuck out a few inches. With expert ease, he crimped the blasting cap using his teeth, affixing the fuse. He ran it off the spool as he backed away.

"How far do we go?"

"I ain't stayin' in this 'ere mine, not if that much dynamite's gonna go bang," Rick said. "Cut about two feet. Burns a foot a minute, that'll give us plenty of time to clear the 'ell out."

"What about the others?"

"They have their own schedules," Rick said.

"I don't think anybody should be in the mine when even one detonation goes off. Rourke had said he wanted all the blasts to go off together." Slocum looked at the shaky timber holding up the roof. More than one crack ran through the walls deep into the mountainside. Even one misplaced charge could collapse the shaft.

"Then go on out and let Shameless know we're gonna blow it," Rick said.

Slocum trotted toward the mouth of the mine. It was dark outside, but over near the gold vault he caught sight of a miner's light bobbing about. He slowed when he got closer to the mouth. Cold air blew against his face—and carried two hoarse voices.

"We kin do it, I tell you. Won't take much dynamite, and we got half a crate. We blow right on through the wall. We can take all the gold 'fore anybody's the wiser."

Slocum didn't hear the reply, but the men argued. He took off his miner's light and aimed it at the ground as he stepped closer to the mouth. The voice definitely came from the direction of the light dancing around on the vault wall.

"We cover it by blowing when the big charge goes off in the main shaft," said a voice Slocum almost recognized. Distance and wind robbed it of real recognition.

"Won't be that long. We kin mark it and . . ." The man's voice trailed off. Slocum heard only whispers and then nothing. He took a couple more steps and emerged from the mine, to see if he could identify the men plotting to rob Snell of his gold.

Slocum threw up his arm to shield his eyes when the miner's lamp was directed into his eyes. He turned and hastily retreated into the mine. The light disappeared, but he heard more frantic whispering.

". . . kill when he comes out," was all Slocum understood.

He ran back into the mine to warn Rick, and collided with the man so hard that they both bounced back and fell to the ground.

"What you in such a 'urry for, Slocum?" Rick stood and rubbed his butt. "Dang, you mighta busted something important back there. I'm gonna 'ave a bruise—"

"Two men," Slocum got out. He gasped for air. The fall had driven the wind from his lungs. Simply taking a breath felt as if he sucked in razor blades. "Th-they're going to blow up the gold storage and steal the gold."

"Whoa there, partner. Let's talk about this outside."

"Shoot us," Slocum got out, but his voice was too low for Rick to hear.

Slocum did hear the other man say, "I lit the fuse. We've only got a few minutes to get clear."

Slocum got to his feet and went after Rick. He had barely gone a dozen paces when a single shot rang out in the still night. The report echoed down the mine shaft louder than thunder. Slocum spun his miner's lamp up and saw Rick flat on his back, a dark bullet hole in the middle of his forehead.

If Slocum left the mine, that would be *his* fate, too. And if he didn't, the blast would probably kill him.

6

Slocum turned back to the mouth of the mine and saw a glint of light reflected off a blued gun barrel. It was certain death if he tried to leave. The miners waiting outside had killed Rick thinking he had overheard them. Their next murder would eliminate the real threat to their scheme of robbing Snell of his gold.

A bullet sang off a wall to Slocum's right. He flinched and went into a crouch. He turned the carbide lamp down to the floor to keep from making a target of himself. Two more shots followed in the span of a heartbeat. Without a choice, he inched back into the mine, then bolted and ran as hard as he could for the spot where Rick had lit the fuse. He would be killed by the shock wave leaving the mine if he stayed, even if the roof didn't collapse on his head. At best, the dynamite would do its job and blast apart a huge section of rocky wall. The dust would choke him to death before he could ever hope to get clear of the mine.

Another shot lent speed to his retreat. When he slipped around a slight curve in the drift, he lifted the miner's light to better see where he ran. He heard the hissing fuse as he got closer. He had no idea how long it had been since Rick lit the fuse. Slocum went pale when he saw how close the fuse was to burning down to the blasting cap.

Dropping the carbide lamp, he dived and clawed at the now burned fuse. The ash came away in his hand, leaving an ugly black smear. He scrambled, got his feet under him, and lunged again. This time his fingers clamped down over the sizzling spark marching inexorably for the blasting cap and four sticks of dynamite.

The magnesium in the fuse burned his fingers, but he yanked back and pulled the fuse and blasting cap away from the end stick of dynamite.

The cap detonated and knocked him backward into the wall. For a moment the world went black. Then only pain filled him like an overflowing rain barrel.

A sharp pain in the center of his back warned him he had impaled himself on a sharp rock. The burning in his hand cheered him, though. He felt. That meant the blasting cap hadn't taken his hand off when it detonated. Reaching up, he ran his hands over his stubbled cheeks and laughed at the sensation. Rough beard. Fingertips scraping across his skin. He had both hands and had survived.

Slocum sat where he was for another minute, aware of the hot trickle down his back that puddled around his waistline. Finally, getting enough strength, he grunted and lurched forward. The pain almost blacked him out. He supported himself on his hands, then got to his hands and knees and finally struggled to his feet.

He retrieved his miner's lamp and fastened its loop around his head to see what had happened. His last-instant yank had saved his life from the dynamite blast. He pulled the fourth stick of explosive from the hole and stared at it for a moment. Knowing what he had to do, he found the spare caps they had brought, and cut off a few inches of miner's fuse to make a new bomb.

He returned to the mouth of the mine. Rick still lay where he had fallen. Outside, he couldn't tell if the would-be thieves were waiting for him to poke his head out, or if they had turned tail and run. Slocum applied the end of the fuse to the carbide and set the fuse to sputtering. Only then did he leave the mine. He looked around to see if anybody lay in ambush.

Men walked from another shaft, dragging their tools with them. He rocked back to throw the dynamite, and then stopped when Seamus Rourke bellowed at him.

"Don't, Slocum. Don't throw the dynamite! You'll kill ever'body!"

The foreman led the men coming from the next mine shaft. Slocum lowered his deadly bomb and tried to locate the men who had killed Rick. The camp was shrouded in darkness. Nobody moved but miners coming from the bowels of the earth.

He plucked out the fuse and tossed it away. Then he dropped to his knees, all strength gone from his legs.

"What 'n the bloody hell's goin' on?" Rourke demanded. He grabbed the stick of dynamite from Slocum and heaved it into the night. "You gone plumb crazy?"

"Rick's dead, Boss," came a fearful voice. "Deader 'n a doornail."

"You killed him, Slocum," Rourke said. "You son of a bitch. He was a good man and you killed him."

"No, I didn't," Slocum said. He fought to keep from passing out. His entire back was afire. The way he felt meant that the wound still gushed blood. If he didn't get tended to soon, he would bleed to death. "Shot. Somebody trying to steal the gold. Shot Rick. Tried to kill me."

He keeled over and crashed facedown to the ground. The next thing he remembered was the return of excruciating pain all over his back.

In the distance came a voice he recognized.

". . . never woulda thunk it of him. Seemed a decent fellow."

"Snell," Slocum called out, but his voice was caught in his throat. His mouth was filled with cotton, and he could hardly force his eyes to flutter open.

"He shot Rick smack between the eyes and then tried to

blow up the rest of us," Rourke said hotly. "He had a lit stick of dynamite in his hand when we caught him."

"Where's the six-shooter?"

"What?" Rourke looked at Snell as if he had grown a second head. "I don't follow."

"'Course not, you blithering idiot. He had dynamite in his grubby hand. Where's his six-shooter?"

"He musta dropped it. Hid it."

"Windsor," Snell said tiredly. "Go to the bunkhouse and paw through Slocum's belongin's and tell me if you find a six-gun that's been fired."

Windsor took off at a run. Snell ran his hand over Slocum's back. Slocum winced at the pain.

"Don't know what you got yerse'f into, Slocum, but it's a nasty bit of work. You damn near ran yerse'f through and through, but we got you patched up."

"Didn't kill Rick," Slocum grated out. The pain made the room dance all around him, and the heat spreading up and down his spine set him on fire.

"We're checkin' into that. Here's Windsor." Snell disappeared from Slocum's blurry field of vision, but he heard the mine owner and foreman talking.

"Ain't been fired. His six-gun was still in its holster in the bunkhouse," Windsor said.

"He coulda replaced it," Rourke said, surly now.

"I said you were a blithering idiot. Don't make me hunt fer words even worse. When could he? You and the rest of the boys knocked him down as he came out of the mine. I sent some of them to hunt, but there's no sign of a gun anywhere around the mine him and Rick was in. Somebody else shot Rick. Don't reckon they did this to Slocum."

Slocum winced as Snell pressed his fingers into the wound on his back. He felt wetness forming on the bandages. The mine owner had opened the puncture again.

"See that he's got new bandages. That's a mighty bad wound. Surprised he even stood up, much less waved around a stick of dynamite."

Slocum heard Snell and Rourke arguing as they left. Windsor remained to peel off the soaked bandages and to put new ones around Slocum. The foreman did a better job than Snell. Slocum thanked him.

"No reason to thank me. I'd do it for any of you cayuses. What happened in there?"

Slocum started to tell him, then decided he would only risk getting himself killed like Rick if he made a mistake and Windsor was in on the planned theft. Only Snell was safe to tell all he had overheard.

Slocum's mind turned over the problem facing him, and he realized he couldn't say anything about what he had overheard to anyone. If Snell wasn't the full owner of the Shady Lady Mine, he might be planning on robbing the gold to do his partners out of their share. The time he had spent with Snell didn't quite convince him the man was honest. Chances were good that he was a square shooter, but Slocum was too weak and confused to know anything for certain.

"Need to sleep," he said. He didn't sleep so much as pass out. When he came to, sunlight slanted through a window onto his bed. He tried to sit up, but found he was too light-headed to make it on the first try. Bracing himself against the side of the bed, he levered up to a sitting position and waited for the room to stop spinning around and around.

"You gettin' yer strength back?"

Slocum rubbed his eyes and saw Snell sitting at a table across the room. Papers were strewn all over. It took him a few seconds to realize he had spent the night in the mine owner's bed.

"Need some coffee. Stronger the better."

"Don't let the cook hear you say that. He makes coffee so strong a spoon melts in it."

"What I need."

"You up to tellin' me what went on?"

Slocum studied Snell and tried to figure out if the man deserved the truth. He did, but Slocum was too wary to pass it along. He would keep his ear to the ground and find the men responsible for the planned thievery.

"Got mixed up. Rick lit the fuse too early, I went back, something happened. He got shot. I pulled the fuse loose in time to stop the blast."

"Just as well," Snell said. "That vein runs through mighty hard rock. You mighta brung down the whole shaft or done nuthin' more 'n scratchin' the rock. I looked. I think the rock's too hard for dynamite."

"Too hard? Four sticks."

"I got me other plans. But what I want to know is why'd Rick git shot? Who did it?"

Slocum shook his head. It felt as if important parts rattled loose inside. He waited for the pain and dizziness to pass. "Might be he had enemies in camp. I haven't been here long enough to know about that."

"He was a friendly galoot. Hard to think anybody held a grudge against him what didn't come right on out and say so. Rick'd smooth it all over. He was that kind of man."

"You fetching the marshal?" Slocum tried to stand, but his legs were rubbery and tried to fold up under him. He sat back onto the bed, sweating now at the notion of Snell getting Marshal Pritchard in from Sage Junction to investigate Rick's murder.

"No need. The town marshal over in Border don't know his ass from a hole in the ground. Me and Windsor and Rourke will poke about and wait fer the guilty party to confess. They always do." He held up a dime novel. "Leastways, they always do in these. A steely eyed stare's 'nuff to break the meanest man's will." Snell tossed the cheap novel onto the table, where it scattered papers. He grumbled as he straightened them. "I declare, there's more papers to file than rock to dig."

"I'll get on back to the bunkhouse. I can rest up for the evening shift," Slocum said.

"Stay put. There's not likely to be much in the way of work tonight. The two tunnels that set off their charges didn't bring up any ore worth diggin'. The tunnel Rick and you was in, now, that's where I'm puttin' my money on finding the mother lode."

"I can be ready to work tonight's shift."

"I'm spendin' a purty penny for some professional blastin' tonight. You curl up, and I'll be sure to roust you when your shift's on," Snell said.

"Thanks."

"Don't think I'm givin' up my bed two nights in a row. Danged near broke a bone sleepin' on a cot over in the bunkhouse." Snell made one last futile attempt to corral the papers on the table, stood, and left Slocum sitting on the edge of the bed.

Slocum considered going to the table, pawing through the papers, and trying to find out if Snell might be cheating his partners. Instead, he laid back down and was asleep within minutes.

This time when he awoke, the sun was setting and cold wind whipped down from higher elevations, snaked through the walls, and poked at him. Slocum stirred, stretched carefully, and felt the skin on his back stretch enough to give him a twinge. The lack of pain heartened him. He bent over, pulled on his boots, and then, moving slowly, he stood and made his way to the bunkhouse to get his spare shirt. By the time he reached the mess hall, the men had finished their dinner.

"Here," Windsor said, pushing a plate of beans with a sad-looking hunk of corn bread on the side in his direction. Slocum settled down and pulled the food the rest of the way in front of him. He began eating slowly, then with greater appetite as he realized it had been more than a full day since he had seen any food.

"You killed Rick, didn't you?" asked Rourke.

Slocum didn't bother looking up from his plate to deny it.

"Why'd you go and do it? The two of you have an argument? You ain't been in camp long enough to owe money or be owed."

"Somebody else shot him," Slocum said, using a morsel of corn bread to mop up the last of the beans. He considered getting more, but his strength wasn't up to the task. He wondered how he was going to put in a full shift.

"Rick was a sociable fellow. Everybody liked him."

Slocum said nothing about the reason Rick had been gunned down. The two men planning on blasting their way into the gold storage warehouse had mistakenly thought Rick had overheard them. In a way, Slocum owed Rick. He had been killed for no reason other than to shut Slocum up.

For the first time since he had stumbled out of the mine, Slocum was fed, rested, and almost free of pain. The thought popped into his head that he might still be a target—unless the gold thieves mistakenly thought that Rick had been the one spying on them. If Slocum was in their boots, he'd try to kill anybody who might let the cat out of the bag. More than the wound on his back, he would be walking around the mining camp with a bull's-eye there.

He was stuck here until he got money for a horse, unless he wanted to steal one of Snell's lop-eared mules. He had been forced to ride the ornery critters on occasion. They were sure-footed, tireless—and slow. A man on foot could overtake him if a mule took it into its brain to saunter along.

Slocum began turning over other schemes in his head, ignoring Rourke's stream of accusations. He wasn't likely to get far walking. Hell, he could barely stand. A desperate notion came that might work, if he could identify the thieves. If he threw in with them, he could get out of camp along with the gold. They had to have some plan for making off with several hundred pounds of gold bars, and he could use that to get away from the Shady Lady Mine.

A slow smile came to his lips. He might even cut himself in on the gold. The smile faded when he realized Snell would call in the marshal from Border, and probably every lawman within a hundred miles. For all his easygoing ways, Snell wasn't the sort to let a mountain of gold slip through his fingers and not demand justice.

When Marshal Pritchard got wind of the theft, whether Slocum helped or not, he would identify Slocum right away.

"What's Snell planning for the night shift?" Slocum asked.

This cut off Rourke's tirade. The foreman opened his mouth, but no words came out. He clamped it shut, glowered, and then finally answered.

"Said he was bringing in a blasting expert. We kin do the blasting ourselves. He don't need no outsider."

"From Salt Lake City?" Slocum considered how a specialist in mining engineering would travel. Maybe he came in a buggy loaded with his own equipment. If so, he had a horse pulling the rig. If he drove something heavier, chances were good he had a team of horses. Stealing one meant that by sundown tomorrow Slocum could put forty miles between him and the pair of miners intent on plugging him.

"Don't know. Snell don't tell me much, not like he does Windsor."

Slocum heard the bitterness in Rourke's tone, and wondered if the second-shift foreman might be part of the plot to steal Snell's gold. Rourke's insistence that Slocum had killed Rick made more sense if the man was involved in relieving the vault of its metallic load.

Walking slowly at first, Slocum let his muscles find their own way of moving until his stride was strong and he looked the pinnacle of health. He only wished he felt better.

"Gather 'round, men," called Snell. His eyes fixed on Slocum for a moment; then the mine owner nodded slowly in approval. "We got a genuine expert on blowin' things up to help out in the mines. He's invented a new kind of explosive that's ten times more powerful than dynamite, and he's testin' it in the Shady Lady Mine."

"We kin scrabble out our own gold," muttered Rourke from behind Slocum. "Don't need outsiders comin' in to turn big rocks to little ones."

Slocum edged to the side to put his back to open spaces. He doubted Rourke would shoot him in the back with the entire mining company gathered, but a little caution now might save his life.

Slocum felt it before he heard it. The ground trembled beneath his feet; then part of a mountain at the far end of the compound exploded upward, showering them all with dust and small rocks. He was turned away from the blast, so he was only pelted with pebbles. Others were not as lucky. One miner caught a flying rock chip in his eye and yelped like a scalded dog. The assembly of miners milled about, knowing what a premature blast meant in the mine.

"Settle down, boys. It's jist fine. That there was a sample of what he kin do."

Through the dust cloud emerged a fancy-dressed man on a prancing stallion. The rider was decked out in an expensive coat and had fancy hand-tooled boots that caused a snicker among the miners. Nobody but a greenhorn ever wore anything so gaudy.

They laughed at the rider, but the young man had a haughty expression. He obviously thought he was far superior to anyone grubbing a living out of a mine. He looked down his nose at them and sneered.

"Only a half pound," he said.

"What's that, mister?" Rourke pushed past Slocum to get closer. "What are you goin' on about?"

"Only a half pound of my explosive reduced an entire mountain to rubble. I am here to solve your blasting problems."

"Ain't had any problems till you showed up," Rourke said angrily.

Slocum ignored the exchange as the rider approached. He had recognized him immediately.

Snell's explosives expert was none other than the youngster Stanford Allen had been whaling away on back at the Crazy Eights Saloon—the kid Slocum had stood up for, only to get his ass fired.

7

"I am Lawrence Greeley, master detonator!" The young man stood in the stirrups and raised a fist as if he challenged the night sky. From where Slocum stood, the rising moon formed a halo behind Greeley's head, making him look like a supernatural being.

A few of the miners snickered, but most kept a respectful silence. Snell turned and raised his hand to quiet the murmurs.

"This here's the best damn chemist west of the Mississippi," Snell called out. "He's got the stuff we need to plow right on through the mountain and into tomorrow, gatherin' gold nuggets as we go."

"With only a few ounces of my new explosive, I can do the work of a dozen crates of your old dynamite."

"There's nuthin' wrong with dynamite," groused Rourke. "Beats the hell out of blasting powder."

"Blasting powder," scoffed Greeley, "is ancient science. I will condemn dynamite to the same dustbin of history with my newer, more powerful energetic!"

"Energetic? I thought you had a new explosive," said Rourke.

Greeley laughed sarcastically and turned from the night-shift foreman. He addressed the others, who stood in hushed awe of his fancy-ass claims.

"For my paltry fee, I will make the Shady Lady Mine the most productive in all Wyoming. You need only detonate a pinhead-sized mote to do the work of a half dozen old sticks of dynamite. It is safer, easier to use, and if you like, I can smear it on a wall and blow the entire rock face without drilling."

"You smear that gunk on? And it still blows up?"

Slocum didn't see who asked the question. He was more interested in how the rising moon turned Lawrence Greeley's face into a profile lost in shadow. There was something familiar about the sweep of the nose, the rise of the cheekbones, the slope of the forehead.

"Sarah Beth," he said, catching his breath. Lawrence Greeley looked enough like the woman to be her brother.

"My crew will be here in a few minutes to begin the night's work."

"Why not do the blasting during the day?" Rourke asked.

"I have just arrived. There is no reason to wait for sunlight when the work is done in the pitch darkness of a mine shaft," Greeley said. "There. There's my crew now."

Slocum heard the clank of chains, the creaking of leather, and the straining of horses. A wagon rattled into view and drew up beside Greeley. Slocum stood a little straighter when he saw who rode beside the driver. He had been right about the family resemblance. Sarah Beth sat proudly in the wagon, staring at Lawrence Greeley with more than mere admiration.

Slocum pushed through the miners and tried to circle the wagon to come up on the far side to speak with Sarah Beth. She hadn't noticed him yet, but Greeley had. From his perch atop the powerful stallion, the young man pointed directly at Slocum and said, "You will help with tonight's test firing."

"Go on, Slocum. I need somebody who can keep his head and tell me if that danged stuff works like he claims," said Snell. The mine owner started to slap Slocum on the back and caught himself in time. "He only lets one of my men at a time into the mine with him and his crew. Wish it coulda been me, but you're a sharp-eyed son of a bitch. Don't let me down." Slocum sagged a little when Snell did put his hand on his shoulder. Even this small contact sapped Slocum's strength.

"All I need from you is to observe," Greeley said, swinging his leg over and dropping to the ground. He was shorter than Slocum remembered, giving him even more the appearance of a boy in his teens rather than an adult. Closer, Slocum saw how Greeley was trying to grow a mustache. The dark wisps were hardly more than a smudge on his upper lip.

"How long you been growing that?" Slocum asked.

"What are you talking about?" Greeley knew because he reached involuntarily to run his finger across his upper lip. He glared at Slocum, and for a moment Slocum thought he was going to choose someone else.

"I know you," Greeley said. "You were the bouncer at the saloon in Sage Junction."

"You've got a good memory," Slocum said. "I kept Allen from whaling the tar out of you. From the way he was knocking you around, I'm surprised you saw anything but a fist coming at your face."

"He was a lowlife who deserved what he got. Come along."

Slocum started to balk and call out to Sarah Beth, but the woman had disappeared. He looked around, but didn't see her anywhere. Greeley prodded him painfully, and forced him toward the mine where they were going to detonate.

"You are supposed to be Snell's observer. Keep your eyes peeled. What we're about to do will amaze you." Greeley looked sideways at Slocum. "Why were you working as a bouncer if you're a demolitions expert?"

"Can't say I'm an expert, but I know something about dynamite and mining," Slocum said.

"No one's more of an expert than I am," Greeley said, puffing up. He tried to walk on the balls of his feet to give himself a few extra inches of height, but Slocum still towered above him. He gave up and sank back to the three inches he got from the boot heels. "I am nothing less than a genius," the young man went on. "Harvard had nothing to teach me about chemistry. I should have been the one teaching, not those lackwits who called themselves professors. In my first year, I found the secret formula I am going to demonstrate."

"The same explosive you used up in the pass leading into Sage Junction?" Slocum asked.

"Of course it is, you dolt. Who else could create such a blast? I was testing with only a few ounces, hardly more than I used to reduce that pathetic hill north of here to rubble a few minutes ago."

Slocum let Greeley brag on. He had a good answer now to why Sarah Beth had questioned the settlers about what they had seen. She wanted to know if any of them connected her brother with the explosion. From what Slocum had gathered from the girl, they had been shaken by the blast, as he had been, but had not spotted anyone nearby. Lawrence Greeley had done his test and gotten away with it unseen. Why did he care if the entire world knew he was blasting? Slocum scratched his stubbled chin and walked faster to keep up with the shorter man, whose legs pumped hard now to get them to work.

Slocum ducked as he went into the mine. This was a larger shaft, more than wide enough for him to stick out his arms and not have his fingers brush either wall. Greeley plunged ahead, relying on the light from the lanterns his two assistants carried to show the way. Slocum picked up a carbide lamp for his own use. It seemed that Greeley was a bit contemptuous of the powerful explosive he had invented. Being able to see in the mine should anything go awry seemed more important than ever to Slocum after all that had happened the night before.

"There, see?" Greeley had stopped some distance into the mine and pressed his hand against a sheer rock wall. "This is the vein of quartz Snell wants blasted free." Greeley stepped back as far as he could and studied the hard rock. "This will be easy. Give me an ounce, no more."

One assistant opened a small box, and withdrew a small piece of what looked like gray putty and handed it to his boss. Greeley took it, smashed it flat between his palms, and began pressing it hard against the wall. It stuck like glue.

"Where will the blast be directed? Not you, you idiot. Him. Slocum. Tell me!"

Slocum stepped closer and shone the purplish light from his miner's lamp on the putty. Rather than stuck against the wall, it had been smeared in a pattern circling one specific point.

"If I had to drill a hole for dynamite, smack in the center of that ring's where I'd go." He tapped the bull's-eye. "It looks as if the blast will go down into the wall rather than out from a drilled hole."

"There's hope for some of you cretins," Greeley said. "That's about right. You need more for this to work. You need—"

"Something to press into the wall to keep the blast from coming back rather than going down into the rock," Slocum finished. Greeley glared at him with a look approaching hatred.

"Yeah, right," the young man said. He snapped his fingers, and the two assistants came up with heavy timbers and a sheet of wood a half inch thick. One held the sheet up while the other braced the timbers against it, holding it firmly against the wall. When the sheet was held securely enough, both men went to work putting even more braces into place.

"Looks like you're trying to support the entire mountain with that," Slocum observed.

"There will be a new tunnel behind that sheet of wood."

Greeley imperiously motioned his men away. They left

equipment from a box for him to paw through. He drew out what looked like telegraph cable, and used a penknife to whittle away insulation until bright copper wire was exposed. Greeley twisted about and shoved the wire up under the wood. He used a second piece of wire on another section.

"Unspool the wire. Don't dislodge the electrodes."

"Electrodes?"

"Never mind, Slocum," Greeley said. "You wouldn't understand. This transcends chemistry and goes to electricity."

"The stuff in lightning?"

Again, Greeley fought to hide his surprise.

"Something like that. Consider this to be electricity caught and held to do my bidding."

The wire unwound from the two spools as Slocum backed from the mine. In a few minutes, they were once more under the bright moon and the scattering of stars in the nighttime sky. Greeley bustled around, making fine speeches that mostly were self-laudatory. Slocum looked for Sarah Beth, but the woman was nowhere to be seen.

"I have a special box. A generator of electricity," Greeley said, motioning to an assistant to bring over a small box with a handle on top. Slocum had seen similar devices used by a railroad crew blasting through a rocky patch in the Nebraska prairie. The handle was lifted and when depressed, set a wheel spinning inside. Slocum wasn't sure what happened, but sparks often jumped from the sides of the box.

"Attach the wires," Greeley said, as if making a profound pronouncement. His assistant fumbled while getting insulation off one of the telegraph wires. Greeley pushed him out of the way, cursing his ineptitude.

Greeley drew a penknife with a flourish, stripped the insulation, and then twisted the wire around a post atop the box. He repeated the procedure with the second wire, then stood, hand high above his head.

"I will now show how to blast a mine." He made a flourish, then grabbed the handle and pushed it down fast. From inside the box came a whining sound followed by sparks. Then the ground shuddered and an instant later, the mouth of the mine belched dust and debris. Greeley stood in the hurricane blast like a statue. Covered in dirt, he turned and addressed the assembled miners.

"You may now fetch your gold!"

"Danged fool," mumbled a miner near Slocum. "Didn't even check to see if ever'body was outta the mine 'fore blastin'. Coulda kilt a couple stragglers and never know it."

"Go on, men. See how good the explosive worked," urged Snell.

"You, too, Slocum," said Greeley. "You saw how little explosive was used. Tell them."

"Not much more than a walnut-sized lump," Slocum said. "He knows his job." The compliment came grudgingly. It rankled when Greeley laughed at him.

Slocum joined the miners at the mouth of the mine in time to see Rourke stumbling from the interior. He held up a pair of rocks the size of his fists.

"Gold. He exposed the vein with 'nuff gold to keep us workin' for a month!"

A cheer went up. Rourke got his crew formed up and sent them into the mine. Slocum heaved a sigh. It was time for him to get to work. He picked up a shovel, but Snell stopped him before he joined the others.

"I need a word with you," Snell said. "Tell me what went on 'fore the blast."

Slocum described the process, and emphasized how little of Greeley's explosive had been used.

"Sets it off with 'lectral-icity," said Snell. "Heard tell about this."

Slocum said nothing. He'd had similar experiences, but not with such powerful explosives.

"He worth the price he's chargin'?" Snell asked.

"I don't know what you're paying him," Slocum said, "but if he saves you a shift of drilling and a couple crates of dynamite, he's worth it."

"Claims he is chargin' next to nuthin' fer his services since he wants to experiment." Snell nodded, coming to a conclusion. "He's worth his keep. Two more blasts and we got the whole damn vein exposed. That's a week or more work fer two entire shifts, and he can set and blast in an hour." Snell left Slocum standing with the shovel in his hand to talk with Lawrence Greeley.

As far as Rourke knew, if he even cared, Slocum was still with the mine owner. This gave Slocum the chance to go hunting for Sarah Beth. She had ridden into camp and the wagon was still there. He wanted to talk with her. Dropping the shovel, he headed for the mess hall and found her sitting inside, holding a cup of coffee between her hands.

"He's your brother," Slocum said. She looked up, startled.

"I saw no reason to mention that, John. What would be the point?"

He sat on the other side of the table. She clutched the tin coffee cup even harder and shrank back from him.

"You married?"

Again, he startled her. She took a drink and eyed him over the rim of the cup. When she put the coffee back onto the table, her shock was gone and her bright blue eyes danced.

"Does that matter to you?"

"Might."

"I'm not married. I help Lawrence with his work, what little he permits. I have nothing to do with those odious assistants of his. He has such a low opinion of everyone else."

"Shows he doesn't have good sense then," Slocum said. "He should have a very high opinion of his sister."

"Do you?"

"Is he really so smart?"

"Oh, yes," she said. "Lawrence is brilliant, a true genius. He was only sixteen when he went to Harvard, and he was far more accomplished than his professors."

"Accomplished enough to blow up the Crazy Eights Saloon?"

"You're not a dull boy yourself," she said. Sarah Beth finished her coffee and belched. "Oh, excuse me. That is strong coffee."

"He killed Allen in the blast," Slocum went on. "You knew he had committed the crime and busted me out of jail because you felt guilty about seeing another man take the blame."

"That's a bit dramatic. Couldn't I have freed you because you were . . . you?"

"No," Slocum said firmly. "You won't turn him over to the marshal because he's your brother, but you've got enough starch not to want another man to be falsely accused."

"They were talking about lynching you. That horrid bartender stirred them up. I don't know why he was so keen on blaming you when it was obvious you had nothing to do with either the fire or the death."

"Morgan just might have other reasons," Slocum said. "He was probably stealing from Allen, and wanted to be sure nobody pointed a finger at him. I was handy, nothing more."

"He was quite vocal about seeing you and his employer fighting."

Slocum nodded.

Sarah Beth caught her breath, then let it out slowly. Slocum appreciated the way her breasts rose and fell when she did this.

"You fought over Lawrence, didn't you? You stopped Allen from thrashing him, and Allen threatened to fire you!"

"I quit. Allen was a bully and took too much pleasure whaling away on anybody weaker."

"Lawrence isn't weaker. He proved that. Oh, his stature is a problem for him, but his intellect is gigantic. Allen should never have crossed him."

"It cost him his life and damned near burned down the entire town. All that saved it was the way it had rained all night long." After the way the citizens of Sage Junction had treated him, Slocum thought for a moment that it would have served them right if the town had burned down around their ears. But what Lawrence Greeley had done was wrong. It wasn't any different from shooting a man in the back.

"He didn't mean to kill Allen. I'm sure of that," Sarah Beth said, as if reading his mind. "All Lawrence wanted was to get even. Blowing up the saloon would have been that. It was bad luck that anyone was hurt."

Slocum wanted to believe that for Sarah Beth's sake, but he had seen how full of himself Greeley was. It wasn't much of a leap from thinking he was the smartest man around to believing he was better than everyone else.

"Where are you staying?" Slocum asked.

"Oh, Lawrence wants to pitch camp at the far end of the mining site by the hill he leveled as a demonstration."

"I'll walk you back," Slocum said.

"Very well, but there's no way we . . ." Sarah Beth blushed and looked away. Slocum almost laughed at her sudden shyness.

He didn't even take her arm as they walked to the camp where several tents had already been pitched. Greeley's assistants had been busy. One worked to bring water from the creek a hundred yards away that supplied the miners.

"This is my tent," she said. Sarah Beth looked around. The man lugging buckets of water had dumped them into a trough and walked back to the creek. No one else was in sight. Sarah Beth put her hands on either side of Slocum's head and pulled him down to give a quick, unsatisfying kiss. She pulled away, licked her lips, and started to say something. Common sense overcame her and she left him without saying a word.

Slocum watched her disappear behind the tent flap, and almost followed. Then common sense visited him, too. The time and place were all wrong. He started back toward the mine. He still worked for Snell and the mine owner deserved a decent shift's labor from him.

Before he had gotten halfway to the Shady Lady's main

shaft, Slocum saw three men bathed in moonlight in the middle of the road leading away from the mine. He identified Lawrence Greeley immediately. The man was a full head shorter than the other two. If that wasn't good enough, moonlight reflected like silver off his fancy boots. Greeley was poking his finger into another man's chest. The man brushed the hand away as if shooing away flies.

Slocum frowned, trying to remember where he had seen the man before. Then it came to him. While searching for wanted posters with his own likeness, he had seen another for a bank robber. He couldn't remember the outlaw's name, but the reward had been a hefty five hundred dollars.

An explosives expert and a bank robber arguing at a lucrative gold mine.

Slocum went back to work, mulling over what that pair was up to. Only one answer kept popping up. Slocum wondered if they knew they had competition from a couple miners for the Shady Lady Mine's gold bars.

8

"Keep at it, men," Rourke bellowed. "We got a new drift being blasted tomorrow night."

Slocum lifted a shovel filled with loose gravel and tossed it into the skip as it began moving away from him. The mule pulled resolutely, and wouldn't be back for a few minutes. Slocum leaned on the shovel, wiped his forehead with his bandanna, and rested. His back felt closer to normal after two days, but that wasn't what rankled. Sarah Beth had pointedly ignored him since that first night.

Slocum had seen her with her brother and the two assistants, but not with the outlaw he had spotted the night they had arrived. As he had worked, Slocum had tried to remember who the bank robber Greeley talked to might be. It had taken quite a few hours, but he had come up with a name. Slocum would have bet the full amount of the reward that Warren Lester was the man he saw. Wanted posters had notoriously poor drawings. Very seldom did they carry an actual photograph, but something about Lester's bank robbery had stuck with Slocum for close to eighteen months.

He had been drifting through Salinas when he had seen the town marshal leaving his office. Slocum had gone in to paw through the wanted posters to be sure his own face wasn't among them. It was a crime he had committed—and would do again—that had haunted his days since the end of the war. He had returned to the family farm in Calhoun County, Georgia, to recuperate from getting shot by one of William Quantrill's henchmen. More healed than not, he had found himself arguing with a carpetbagger judge over unpaid taxes. The judge had taken a fancy to the property and had come with a hired gunman to seize it from Slocum.

The man had gotten more than he bargained for. Slocum had taken out the judge and his bodyguard and then fled. The wanted poster for killing a federal judge had spread fast, and always presented a worry for Slocum when he went into a new town. Even after all these years, he occasionally found one of the posters. It was always good to check to be sure he wasn't going to get shot down by the law or a zealous bounty hunter over something that had hardly seemed a crime in the Reconstruction South.

But Lester's poster had detailed a vicious crime. He had not been content robbing a bank in Omaha, but had gunned down the bank president, two tellers, and a customer.

Slocum was sure Lawrence Greeley had been talking to the man responsible for gunning down four men.

"Git back to work, Slocum. Snell ain't payin' you to lean on a shovel."

Slocum adjusted his carbide lamp to focus on the shift foreman. Rourke pushed hard on the ore cart to get it back to the end of the track where Slocum could refill it with debris from the blast Greeley had so expertly orchestrated.

"When's the next section going to be blasted out?" he asked Rourke.

"You ain't done with this one yet," Rourke said. His manner softened a mite when he added, "Looks like tomorrow during the day's the best bet. I seen that little tommy-knocker mixin' up a new batch of his witch's brew. Dangedest thing I ever seen. He pours all them chemicals together and stirs 'em a mite, then pours in more clear liquid—and it ain't water—then gets himself a tiny little ball of wax. Said that's what causes all the fuss when he gooses it with electricity."

"That's about right," Slocum said. "He smeared it all over the wall, braced it to contain the blast, and—" His arm swept around, encompassing the entire mine and the new vein exposed by the powerful blast.

"He calls it science. I say it's only a step away from magic. I seen a *brujo* down in Sonora who could—never mind." Rourke snorted. "You cain't git me talkin' and expect not to work. That's not what we're gettin' paid for, either of us."

Slocum went back to loading the skip car for its next trip outside. The piled ore was loaded onto Snell's wagon and taken down into the valley, where the smelter reduced it to a molten glue, skimmed off the gold, and dumped the dross. His thoughts kept coming back to the vault where Snell kept his gold before shipping it to Salt Lake City. Two miners had been intent on blowing a hole in the side of the building using dynamite. Slocum overhearing them had gotten Rick murdered.

Slocum doubted the miners had anything to do with Warren Lester or Lawrence Greeley. It looked more and more as if two gangs were going to steal the same gold, assuming Lester wasn't nosing around for his health. This got Slocum to thinking. When such outlaws collided, opportunities arose—and they were not legitimate ones. He might collect a double reward if they killed each other off, or he might let them shoot it out and then steal the gold himself.

That appealed to him. Either Lester or the miners would take the blame for the theft, and he would have a few pounds of shiny gold metal to celebrate his rapid trip all the way from Denver. He deserved something for all the rowdy-dow he had gone through up till now.

"Break!" shouted Rourke.

Slocum leaned his shovel against the wall and tiredly walked from the mine. Most of the miners ate in the mine, but Slocum had to see the sky and breathe fresh air, no matter that it was icy cold after being in such hot confines. He stepped out and felt the sweaty shirt plaster itself to his body as if it had frozen in place. It invigorated him. He found a spot near the mouth of the mine and sank down to eat his jerky. Barely had he leaned back gingerly, and found a spot where his back wasn't hurting, than he heard soft, quick footsteps approaching.

"Howdy, Sarah Beth," he said without looking up. "What are you doing out so late?"

"John," she said uncertainly. The dark-haired woman came closer, looking downright nervous like a student being bawled out by her stern teacher.

He gnawed on his beef as looked at her. He was glad he had come out to eat his dinner. The open sky was pleasant, but seeing her beauty again set his pulse to racing a little faster.

"You've avoided me the last couple days." He didn't ask it, he stated it. She jerked up and looked right at him.

"Don't interfere, John. Don't. I'm asking you not to."

"Interfere in what?" Slocum tensed. He knew what she was going to say, and wasn't sure he could betray Snell this way. Turning over a harebrained scheme about stealing gold after it had been stolen from the vault was one thing, but being told to look the other way stung.

"Lawrence's experiment is very important to him. He's worried you'll try to discredit him. After all, he showed you how he worked, but he's sure you'll bad-mouth him to Mr. Snell and try to get the experiment called off."

"Snell can make his own decisions," Slocum said. "That hardly matters, though, since I don't have his ear. I just came to work here. He's got two foremen he'd listen to before me. If anyone's trying to stop your brother, it's Rourke or Windsor."

"He's sure you are the one."

"Because I saw him with a bank robber?"

"What?" Sarah Beth jumped as if she had been poked in the ribs with a stick. "I don't understand."

"The night he showed off his explosive, I saw him with an outlaw by the name of Warren Lester. Leastways, he went by that moniker when he robbed a bank in Omaha. A man like that's not content to rob just one bank either. There's probably a long string of robberies and murders to his credit."

"I don't know what you're talking about, John."

Slocum said nothing, but continued to munch on his jerky. She was flustered now. He wanted to see what she did next.

Sarah Beth stared hard at him. Her lips thinned to a razor slash. She abruptly left amid a swirl of her skirts. Slocum watched her stalk off, and wondered if he would ever see her again. He reckoned he had touched a sore spot mentioning Warren Lester. It made him wonder about the rest of Greeley's assistants. No man could keep up with all the wanted posters floating around the West, even when some had his own picture on them.

Slocum gnawed off another plug of jerky and took a swig of water as he heard boots crunching in the gravel. He looked up to see Seamus Rourke with fists clenched and blood in his eye.

"You been talkin' to Greeley's sister?"

Slocum nodded. There was no reason to dispute it since Rourke obviously knew. Since Sarah Beth had gone in the direction of the mine, she must have sought out the foreman and vented her anger about how Slocum had bad-mouthed her brother. He wondered if she had included how he had done it, or if even mentioning that any of her brother's acquaintances were wanted by the law might expose a plot she was involved in.

Slocum considered his cynical assumption that Sarah Beth and Lawrence Greeley were both involved in a plot to steal the gold pulled from the Shady Lady Mine. He was getting suspicious of everyone.

"You don't do that again, Slocum. You hear?"

"Any reason?"

"She said you were forward, made unwanted advances. Ain't grounds to fire you, but I swear I'll work your ass so hard, you won't have any time to bother a pretty filly like her again."

"I'm here to work," Slocum said, getting to his feet. His muscles ached from the hard work and his back twinged a mite, but otherwise, he was in good condition.

"Into the mine. I got a special job for you."

Slocum didn't like the sound of that, but had no reason to quit. If he did, it was a long walk to Border, and even longer getting away from Marshal Pritchard, if the Sage Junction lawman still hunted for him. By now, all the lawmen in the area had to know a murderer was being sought. He was sorry he hadn't given a summer name to Snell when the mine owner had asked.

"All the way to the back of the mine. I want you to clear a spot along the rock face exposed by the blast."

Slocum trudged a quarter mile into the mine and found the spot Rourke had indicated. Greeley's blast had drilled to one side off the main shaft, but this area had been cracked open to expose yet another vein of gold. The whole damned mountainside was filthy with the glittery metal. Slocum poked about with his shovel, then began loading the ore cart. This went on for close to an hour. Nobody came to spell him or talk to him. Usually, Slocum wasn't much for palaver on the job, but he found the isolation wearing on him now. Snell had rightly pointed out how most of the miners were like magpies, always chattering away about anything and everything.

When he got the skip car loaded, he pushed it to a juncture, closed off the tracks, and took an empty car from a short siding. By the time he returned with another laden cart, the first was empty and waiting for him. The work was hard, and he sweat off a couple pounds in the hot mine. He had expected it to be cold underneath the mountain, but the opposite occurred. He guessed there might be a hot-water river running somewhere nearby through the rock. If so,

Greeley was lucky he hadn't ruptured the subterranean channel, or he would have flooded the mine good and proper.

As Slocum finished mucking the last of the stone from the floor, he leaned against the ore cart and played his miner's lamp over the wall at the end of the shaft. Glinting specks of gold appeared everywhere. Some might be fool's gold embedded in the quartz vein, but he didn't think so. He had enough experience to tell the difference between iron pyrite and the real metal.

"You finished?" Rourke asked. Slocum looked over his shoulder. The foreman had come up on him carrying a miner's candle rather than wearing his brilliant carbide lamp.

"Cleared the end of the shaft," Slocum said.

"Good. Now blast out three or four feet."

"I need to drill a hole for the dynamite," Slocum said. Then he faced Rourke and asked, "Why not have Greeley blow it? That tiny dab of explosive he uses would be better."

"He can blast at right angles to the shaft. Needs to brace where he puts the explosive. This here's at the end of the shaft. There's nothing to contain his blast."

"So you want this to be done using regular explosives?"

"And you're gonna do it, Slocum. That oughta keep you busy for another shift or two."

Slocum said nothing.

"Git to it. I'll move this cart outta your way." Rourke came around, kicked away the chock under the metal wheels, and began pushing the cart out. Metallic clanks sounded as he disappeared.

"There's yer tools, Slocum."

Slocum walked a few yards along the tracks and found where Rourke had dropped a drill bit and hammer. He picked them up and returned to the rock face. Drilling was a two-man job. One held the bit and the other swung the heavy sledge. He scratched his head as he walked back and forth in the narrow confines, studying every inch of the rock face.

It was a two-man job if he drove in a single-bore hole. One man could accomplish the same work with four one-stick-deep holes. The sledge was heavy to heft in one hand, but he choked up on the handle, braced the bit with rock, and began hammering until he sank about a foot into the wall. Then he moved to another spot.

The third hole went easily, almost as if he tried to cut through sandstone. Slocum blew away the dust from his drill bit and studied the point carefully. He was no geologist, but this section looked chancy for blasting. Softer than the surrounding rock, it didn't carry the vein of ore Rourke wanted him to follow.

Slocum finished with a fourth hole. All were equally spaced, but the one in the softer rock still bothered him. Slocum took the long walk back and hunted for Rourke to tell him about his concerns. The shift foreman was arguing with two miners and obviously not pleased to see Slocum.

"I told you to get that section finished, Slocum. What are you doin' outside the mine?"

"There's something wrong with part of the rock."

"I don't want excuses. There's nuthin' wrong with rock, unless you mean the rocks you got fer brains. You git that section blasted." Rourke was shouting now.

"You're the boss," Slocum said. He went to the shed where they stored the dynamite. He didn't even have to ask for the sticks of dynamite or caps and fuse. The miner at the shed handed it all over to him.

"You know how to use this here stuff?" the miner asked.

"As good as any here, I suppose," Slocum said. "You ever find any soft rock in the Shady Lady?"

"Soft rock?" The miner laughed. "Ain't nuthin' in that mine but the hardest danged rock in all Wyoming."

"I'm supposed to blast, and there's a part that's softer than the rest."

"No reason for that I kin think of. You need help with the blastin'?"

"Nope," Slocum said.

"You show that fancy-pants greenhorn how to do it. I don't care if he's got explosives a thousand times more powerful than any ole stick o' dynamite. It takes a man to blast, and he ain't much o' one."

Slocum had heard similar sentiments from other miners. They appreciated the ease of use and the stark destructive might of Greeley's invention, but they resented the inventor. He was too arrogant, and obviously held them all in contempt as being beneath him intellectually.

Carrying his equipment in a wood crate, Slocum passed where Rourke was chewing out the two miners. Slocum almost asked one last time about the rock in the mine, then decided the foreman ought to know his job. The long walk to the back of the mine about tired Slocum out. His back ached constantly now, and the work had taken its toll on his strength. If Rourke had let him work with another miner, he wouldn't be in such sorry shape.

If wishes were horses, he would be riding out of Wyoming, heading for Montana or maybe Oregon.

He slid sticks into the four holes he had drilled, tamped in stone around to help contain the blast, then worked to crimp four blasting caps onto three feet of miner's fuse. This gave him three minutes before the blast. He knotted the fuses and ran a couple more feet off in a single fuse. All he needed to do was light this and five minutes later, the dynamite would cave in the back of the mine, exposing more of the precious gold.

Slocum worried his thumbnail on the soft rock one last time, then backed away, struck a lucifer, and set the black fuse to sputtering.

There was no need to run from the mine. He had plenty of time. As he went, he called for other miners to clear out. Being toward the end of their shift, they didn't have to be asked twice. They not only knew the danger of remaining in the mine during a blast, but were ready to quit for the night.

Slocum stepped out into the cold Wyoming night and

took a deep breath. Then he caught and held it when a miner ran up to him and shouted, "Rourke! Rourke's in there."

"The hell you say. I didn't see him."

"He was goin' down one of them galleries that got blasted open. He wouldn't hear you."

Slocum cursed. Only a minute—two at the most—remained before the dynamite detonated.

He ran into the mine shouting at the top of his lungs. Ahead, he saw Rourke struggling to climb out over a pile of rock that hadn't been cleared out yet in a newly blasted section.

"What you goin' on about, Slocum? I tole you—"

"Fire in the hole!" Slocum grabbed the man, pulled him around and shoved him toward the mouth of the mine just as the explosion went off.

Slocum felt the force of the blast lifting and dropping him to the floor. He scrambled to his feet and was caught up by a new danger. Hot water surrounded him like a shroud, buoyed him, and began smashing him from side to side in the mine shaft.

9

Water filled Slocum's mouth and nose, choking him, drowning him. He thrashed about, but the force of the hot water all around him was too great. The scrape of rock as he was catapulted from the mine was almost the last thing he remembered. Pain lanced into his back and water burned in his lungs. Then he was skidding along the rocky ground before he smashed into a heavily laden ore cart.

He blacked out for a moment. When he came to, the world was filled with dancing miners' lights and a babble so loud it deafened him. Then he heard a distant buzz, and realized his hearing had only returned after the earsplitting explosion had robbed him of one of his senses.

Strong arms helped him sit up. He tried to fight, but was weaker than a newborn kitten.

"You all in one piece, Slocum? What the hell happened to my mine?"

"Mr. Snell?" Slocum blinked and got a clearer picture. Snell knelt beside him. Three others peered over the mine owner's shoulder.

"Why did the damned mine blow up like that?"

"Rourke? Did he get out? He told me to blast that wall. Water behind it. Underground river. Soft rock."

"Don't say anything else until you're speakin' straight. Git him some whiskey."

Slocum sputtered as a bottle was forced between his lips. He took a pull, gagged, then took another and let the liquor burn away the last of the cobwebs in his brain. He got out the story of how he had drilled and blasted where Rourke told him.

"Find that stupid son of a bitch. Rourke knows better than to have one man do blastin'. He knows a damn sight better what rock like that means, too."

Slocum sagged back against the ore cart, and looked around for the bottle to take another drink. It was already making the rounds of the miners surrounding him. Now and then he caught the glint of a carbide light off the clear glass. When the whiskey returned to him, the bottle had been drained.

"How're we gonna stop the water from pourin' out?" Windsor stood with his hands on his hips, glaring at the steady flow from the mouth of the Shady Lady.

"You know there's nuthin' to do but wait. Dammit. That's the best vein of gold ore I've found in years," grumbled Snell.

"It's not pouring out anywhere near as fast," Slocum said. He stood up through the force of will. "When the wall breached, the water was under incredible pressure. Now it's only a trickle."

"You think?" Snell shoved Slocum forward. "Let's go see. The water's not boilin', so you won't lose any more skin than you already have. There might be a way to divert the flow."

"Another blast along the shaft," Slocum said, understanding what the owner meant. "A shaft blown downslope will drain it off, away from the new ore."

"You sure you ain't a minin' engineer, Slocum? No, 'course not."

Slocum and Snell waded in knee-deep water that forced them to stumble and stagger along. The flow wasn't too fast, giving Slocum some hope that his scheme might work. He had tried to walk across a fast-running river in ankle-deep water once, and had been swept off his feet. This was difficult to walk in, but not impossible. Clinging to supports, they made their way in.

"Son of a bitch. There's Rourke. Gimme a hand, Slocum."

They went to the foreman, who was curled up in an overturned ore cart. The first blast of water had upended it, and somehow Rourke had found sanctuary inside the cart's hopper. The full force of the rushing water had been broken by the cart, but that didn't mean he was still alive. He might have drowned.

Slocum got a grip under Rourke's arms and heaved the man upright. Rourke sputtered and coughed up some water and began to fight. Slocum let him fall back to the mine floor.

"What the hell went on?" Rourke stared up at Slocum, but didn't see Snell. "You blasted out the end of the mine!"

"You told me to."

"I didn't mean for you to do it tonight!"

"Git him on outta here. I don't think he's up to hearin' what I'm likely to say whilst settin' up to his ass in hot water." Snell snorted and followed the foreman and Slocum out. "Then again, hot water's nuthin' compared to the scaldin' he's gonna git fer bein' so damn stupid."

Slocum shook himself like a dog and sent water spraying in all directions. He stopped when he heard Snell cursing at him.

"Slocum, you blowed up my mine. You kin damn well fix it. You heard what I said. Go blast me a new one!"

Snell stormed off, leaving Slocum standing alone. The other miners gathered in tight knots and whispered among themselves. Windsor finally came over and gave Slocum a disapproving look.

"What's he want from you?"

Slocum explained the idea of blasting a relief channel to divert the water down the hillside, over by the road leading up the mountain.

"I'll see that you get the dynamite. How much do you need?"

"A crate, maybe two. If I find a channel of the soft rock, I can blast the plug out and not need much at all."

"I'll see you get two crates worth." Windsor bellowed his orders and got three miners to help Slocum drill and set the charges. "I'll bring the dynamite down to you."

"Boss, it's the end of the shift," whined a miner. "We ain't done nuthin' to get punished with a double shift. It was Slocum's doin'. Him and Rourke. Make them repair the damage."

Slocum had never heard such sulfurous words flow as he did then. He thought he knew every cuss word ever, but he suspected Windsor made some up as he tied the miners' ears back with his tirade. He stomped off, heading toward Snell's office and quarters.

"He's got a tongue like a razor," said one miner. "What's pullin' a double shift? We git paid."

"We'll be pullin' a triple," groused another. "You don't think they're gonna let us out of tomorrow night's shift 'cuz we worked the livelong day, do you?"

"This might not take too long," Slocum said. "The soft rock is what we need to blow out, and it's like a plug in a tub. If we get lucky, it won't take an hour."

The three miners Windsor had assigned to him as work crew were dubious, but Slocum led them downhill. The rising sun worked in his favor, reflecting off the different strata and allowing him to identify the schist sandwiched between harder layers. When he scraped at one section with his knife, he found the rock was moist. It would only be a matter of time—maybe years—before the underground river eroded its way out of the mountain and cascaded down the mountain at this point. He'd help Nature along with some judicious blasting.

"This is where we need to put the charge," he said, looking around the area. A few small trickles of water leaked from the rock, but he had found the one segment that acted as a plug. Blow it, and the water would leave the Shady Lady Mine two hundred feet above.

"You know what you're doin', Slocum?" The miner scratched himself and looked around for a spot to get in the shade. After working the night shift so long, these men were pasty-white and not inclined to appreciate the sun's warmth on their faces.

"The mine's flooded. This will drain it," he said. He rummaged through the crates of dynamite Windsor had brought down and found what he needed. "Start boring a hole for the explosive here."

"We ain't workin' fer you," complained another. "We got sent here 'cuz Windsor's got a bug up his ass over what you done in the mine."

"Consider it a punishment detail," Slocum said, his voice taking on a steel edge of command. He had been a captain in the CSA and had learned to motivate men who wanted to be somewhere else—anywhere else. During the war, it had been a matter of life or death. Now it was only tired men wanting to find a place to curl up and sleep until their next shift, which would be too soon for any of them.

"You cain't make us," the miner said, coming up. He puffed up his barrel chest and lifted his chin. Slocum didn't even wind up. He just swung. He had been wielding a sledge in the mine enough to turn the proper muscles to steel for such a blow. His fist connected with the point of the man's chin. The miner went down, hitting the ground as stiff as a board.

"Wake him up and get to work," Slocum said. He turned back to preparing the explosive. The other two muttered between themselves, then used some of the water oozing from the side of the mountain to bring around their fallen comrade. The miner sputtered and got to his feet, taking a couple shaky steps in the wrong direction. The other miner who had mouthed off grabbed him and swung him back to the rock where Slocum had ordered them to drill a hole.

By the time Slocum was ready, the miners had a decent hole hammered into the soft rock. He ran his fingers around the rim of the hole, nodded, and said, "Good work. You want to stay around and watch it blow?"

"Why not? We done the work. Ain't never seen an explosion. I mean, we always are outta the mine when the blasts go off."

"Back yonder ought to be far enough," Slocum said, pointing to a spot a dozen yards away. He filled the hole with sticks of dynamite, then placed the rest of the two cases Windsor had given him around, moving rocks to contain the explosion and send its fierce blast directly into the mountainside.

"Fire in the hole!" Slocum lit the fuse and ran.

Something went wrong, terribly wrong. The fuse burned faster and the blast was far more powerful that it should have been. The shock wave caught Slocum and picked him up as if he were a rag doll. He felt his feet pedaling hard, trying to get traction and finding nothing but thin air. When he smashed into a rock, it knocked the wind from him. He lay staring up at the bright morning sky and heard the three miners cackling like hens far in the distance.

"Put him out. He's on fire."

Slocum heard that, but didn't understand. When a miner began rolling him over and over in the dirt, it came to him what the burned smell was. His shirt was on fire, and the tickling sensations on his arms and back were caused by his flesh blistering. Dizzy and gasping for air, he finally stopped turning over and over to lie facedown in the dirt.

"Oughta piss on the bastard to put out the fire," declared the miner he had punched.

"You had it comin'," said another.

Slocum listened to them arguing as he tried to piece together what had happened. By the time he pushed up to his hands and knees and then stood, his head had cleared. A passing vertigo caused him to stumble a few steps; then he went directly for the spot where he had placed the explosive. A torrent of water arched from the side of the mountain.

"At least we drained the mine," Slocum said. He tried to understand how the explosive had detonated so fast and been so powerful. Hobbling over to the spot where he had detonated the dynamite, he found debris hardly larger than gravel. He picked up one piece and rubbed his fingers over the jagged edge.

A waxy residue remained. Slocum sniffed at it and recoiled from the acrid odor.

"What you got, Slocum?"

"The reason I was almost blown to Kingdom Come," he said. He tossed the rock into the stream gushing from the side of the mountain.

"What was that?"

Slocum didn't answer. He had smelled the same scent before—when Lawrence Greeley had detonated his trial blast in the mine. Someone had laced the dynamite with a healthy portion of the more powerful explosive. Slocum had not guessed wrong about how much dynamite to use. He had accidentally used twice the amount needed because of Greeley's more potent chemical.

Somebody had tried to kill him. It might have been a mistake, but Slocum doubted it.

"Who runs the dynamite stores?" he asked.

"Whoever. Folks take turns dolin' out the sticks." The three miners began their trek up the steep road back. Slocum followed more slowly, as much to give himself time to think as to accommodate the aches and pains he was accumulating like a banker hoarded gold coins.

Windsor motioned for the three miners to get some chow and then go to the bunkhouse. Slocum went to the day-shift foreman.

"All blown open. Is the mine draining?"

"Looks to be. Just some damp floor in there. This shift, the muckers won't be working with dry gravel." Windsor shrugged. "That's a small price to pay for gettin' the mine back. You got an eye for blastin', Slocum. If Greeley hadn't come by, I'd want you on my shift."

Slocum tried to hear any note of sarcasm in Windsor's words, and failed to find it. If the foreman had tried to kill him by salting the dynamite with Greeley's explosive, he couldn't tell it.

"Why didn't you just give me some of Greeley's chemical? Wouldn't have taken as much to open the drainage."

He hoped for a rise out of the man, but he didn't see it.

"Greeley keeps a close watch on it. He says he only makes a small batch, and then it's to order. I think he's afraid of it blowin' up on him. I used nitroglycerin a year or two back and I declare, I lost more men on every shift than you can believe. Damned shit is unstable. Shake it just a teeny bit and it'll blow."

"Did you check out the dynamite yourself?"

"What's that? The crates of it you just used? Naw, somebody else was in the shed."

Slocum started to ask who it had been, but he didn't want Windsor to start asking his own questions. The foreman seemed aboveboard, but Slocum couldn't tell. He was bleeding from a dozen new cuts, and the parts of his skin that had blistered began to pain him now.

"I need to get patched up."

"Stood too close to the blast, huh? I'll round up somebody who can sew up the worst of the cuts." Windsor wandered off, shouting at the top of his lungs for someone to help Slocum.

Taking the time, Slocum went to the explosives storage shed and rapped on the door. When he didn't get a response, he shook the door a little. Locked. Whoever had doled out the tainted explosive was long gone. It would be a fool's errand to ask after who had worked in the shed. They'd be like Windsor. Either they hadn't noticed, or they would lie about it.

He limped to the bunkhouse. He was hungry, but needed

rest more. Flopping onto his bunk, he shifted uncomfortably until he found a spot that didn't outright hurt. As he drifted off to sleep, an idea took form in his head, and eventually blossomed into a vivid dream of what he had to do.

The sun was setting when he awoke. Moving was hard because of healing cuts and stiff muscles. He groaned, got out of his bunk, and shuffled to the mess hall.

"Lord Almighty, Slocum, I thought Windsor was lyin' through his teeth about you blowin' yerself up," said Rourke. "We got to catch up on a day lost because of the flood, but I don't want to see you in the mine till you don't look like death's peerin' over yer shoulder. You'll make the other miners edgy, lookin' the way you do."

"Thanks," Slocum said, dropping onto the bench seat. The night shift had eaten already, and the men were gathering tools to begin the work of recovering what they could after the water had carried so much of the gold-bearing ore out of the mine.

"You get some grub and go on back to your bunk." Rourke shook his head, then left.

Slocum wondered at the night foreman's generosity. Most men would have told Slocum to skip dinner and get into the mine or be docked a day's pay for being late to work. He wasn't sure what Snell would have done since the old man had a generous streak in him, but Slocum thought even the mine owner would have ordered him to work. Production had dropped and expenses had mounted. Keeping the steady flow of ore to the smelter was necessary. If the smelter furnace cooled off, it cost a young fortune to fire it up again.

Better to throw in low-grade ore than to let the smelter go idle.

Slocum ate what scraps remained, then heaved to his feet. Resolve hardened in him. He ought to run the hell away from the Shady Lady Mine and he knew it, but someone had tried to kill him. Nobody got away with that.

As he walked into the twilight, he felt stronger and

meaner than ever. He had gone to sleep with a half-baked scheme brewing. When he had awakened, he knew what had to be done. The shift filed into the mine, grumbling as they went. Slocum waited until they were gone and darkness had fallen. It was an hour or more till moonrise. He went to the dynamite shed and rattled the door, testing it. The lock was too secure, but the hasp was barely fastened into the wood. It took only a few minutes of careful work to pry loose the nails holding the metal in the wood and to open the door.

Slocum ducked into the shed and peered around. If it was dark outside, it was blacker than the inside of a grizzly bear's belly within the shed. Rather than leave the door ajar where someone might see it, he closed it, took a gamble, and lit a lucifer. The sulfur tip flared and filled the small shed with an odor that would send any man with common sense running. Fire and explosives didn't mix.

Slocum got his bearings and waited for the match to burn out. He pressed it between thumb and forefinger to be sure it was dead out, then got to work, his hands moving over the crates in front of him. In the dark, he pried off a lid and found the familiar sticks of dynamite resting inside, cradled by sawdust. He took one out, found several blasting caps, and didn't worry about cutting a length of fuse. The blasting caps were sensitive to both fire and pressure, carrying a tiny bead of fulminate of mercury in each one.

He made his way outside, worked to replace the nails he had pried loose. Even a casual inspection would scream out that someone had broken into the shed. Slocum doubted anyone would care, even if the lock fell off in their hands when they opened the door the next time. It wasn't as if Snell had gone out of his way to secure the explosives inside.

As he walked, he examined his stolen treasure for any sign that the dynamite or caps had been altered. The waxy substance Greeley used in his explosive was missing. Slocum wasn't sure if this was good or not. Finding traces on dynamite locked up in the shed meant nothing, since it could have been put there by almost anyone in the mining camp.

Slocum circled the building where Snell stored the gold taken from the mine, mentally ticking off points where he might try to enter to steal the gold, had he been so inclined. The vault was secure enough, but he stopped where he had overheard the two men the other night. He dropped to his knees and examined the building. He found evidence they had been digging there.

He pushed aside a couple rocks and saw how they had burrowed like gophers directly under the building. He wondered what they had stashed under the gold vault. Holes had not been dug anywhere else, making this a special point for some reason.

Slocum did a little digging of his own straight down. He secured the stick of dynamite upright, then put a flat rock on top. Another few minutes of work secured the blasting caps on top of this rock and under another. A thin layer of dirt went over the topmost rock. Anyone stepping down hard, or even kneeling to continue digging, would crush the rocks together, set off the blasting caps and, he hoped, the dynamite beneath.

He was curious to see who turned up dead as a result of his trap.

10

The explosion rocked the bunkhouse and threw Slocum from his bed. He landed hard on the floor, and then covered his head to protect himself from the shower of splinters. One entire wall of the bunkhouse had been blown inward. After a few seconds, Slocum got to his feet and stumbled from the destroyed building. The loss of one wall now caused the other three to collapse. The roof came crashing directly downward. If Slocum had stayed inside, he would have been crushed to death.

He saw a crater in the ground not twenty yards from the warehouse used to store the Shady Lady gold. Slocum started for the vault, and was joined by most of the day shift. From their drunken chatter, they had been in the mess hall playing cards and passing around a bottle of whiskey.

"What happened?" Snell came running out of his house, waving a shotgun around. "We bein' attacked? Injuns again?"

Windsor went to his boss, and the two of them spoke in low tones. Slocum ignored them and went to the vault. To his surprise, his trap was untouched. With so many miners crowding around to find the cause of the blast, he almost dropped to his knees and removed the blasting caps.

"Slocum, what're you doin' here?" Snell still waved his shotgun around, but had calmed a mite.

"I was in the bunkhouse when all hell broke loose," he said.

"You're on the night shift. You're supposed to be workin'."

"Rourke told me to rest after I was almost blown up this morning," he said. Slocum was acutely aware of how his back felt and that it looked like a pound of hamburger.

"I'll have his ears fer that. We gotta work all the men. That means you. I can't have you layin' down on the job."

Snell went off ranting and raving. Slocum pushed his way through the gathered miners to get closer to the crater. By now, miners from the second shift were pouring from the mine, looking around to be sure they weren't in danger. Rourke barked at them to get back to work. They reluctantly obeyed. Then Rourke joined Windsor and Snell on the far side of the crater for a powwow.

All Slocum could see was a four-foot-deep crater. A couple cases of dynamite could have cut such a hole, but he doubted it. He knelt and scooped up a fragment of rock. The sharp edge had blood on it. Somebody had been carrying a whale of a lot of dynamite—or a fist-sized hunk of Lawrence Greeley's potent explosive.

Slocum prowled around, looking at the rocks until he found one smeared with a waxy substance like that he had seen twice before. Somebody had given him a hotshot of dynamite laced with Greeley's explosive. Now a miner had gotten himself blown to hell and gone carrying a large piece of it.

While the miners argued among themselves about what had happened, Slocum made a wide circle of the area. A single set of tracks came in from the direction of Greeley's camp. The rest of the area was too scuffed up by the dozens of miners moving around, but Slocum had a good idea what had happened.

Either Greeley had given one of his men the explosive, or

it had been stolen with the intent of blowing the side out of the gold storage building. Slocum walked directly to Greeley's tent and pulled back the flap.

Greeley stood over Sarah Beth, his hand cocked back to strike her. For a moment, the three of them were frozen. Then Greeley pushed his sister away and stepped back, red in the face with anger.

"What the hell do you want? You can't barge in here," he said.

"Aren't you just a little curious about the explosion?" Slocum asked.

Greeley sneered. "This is a mining camp. They blast all the time. Why should an explosion be worth my time to investigate?"

"Because the dunderhead who got himself blown up was carrying a large chunk of your new explosive," Slocum said. He had hoped to elicit a response from Greeley, and he got one. It wasn't what he expected.

Greeley laughed.

"You think I had something to do with that? I didn't."

"You only mix up the chemicals when you're ready to use the explosive," Slocum said.

"Stay out of my business. Don't go snooping around my workshop. You're not smart enough to understand what's dangerous and what's not."

"I know what's dangerous," Slocum said slowly. "Do you?"

This brought a sputter to the smaller man's lips. He tried to speak, made a gurgling sound, then angrily pushed past Slocum and went outside. Slocum saw Greeley storming toward the crater where someone had died.

"Did he hit you?" Slocum asked Sarah Beth.

"Please, John. Don't get involved. This is a terrible time for Lawrence."

"Yeah, he just lost one of his men. Or was it one of Warren Lester's gang?"

"John, please. Don't." Then Sarah Beth came closer and

reached out to him. Her trembling hand rested on his chest. Slocum wasn't sure if she was going to push him away or pull him closer. His own anger flared when he saw the outline of her brother's hand on her cheek. He reached out and gently touched the livid mark.

He spun and started after Greeley. This time, she did grab him and tugged hard to keep him from going after her brother.

"You don't understand, John. You don't! He's a genius. He . . . he can't control himself sometimes. The genius boils over and infects him and everyone around him and he loses his temper when things aren't going right."

"They don't always go right for him, is that it?"

Sarah Beth shook her head, looking forlorn.

Slocum snorted. He had seen men like this before. The world revolved around them and nothing—and no one else—mattered. For whatever reason, they always had a swarm of men and women with them to make excuses for their behavior.

"You wait here," he told her.

"Don't cross him. He's in a mood right now."

Slocum wasn't listening. He stormed out and hunted for Greeley. The chemist was nowhere to be found. The crater and the body in it were the center of attention for the men in the mining camp. Slocum hoped it had been Warren Lester who had sent pieces of himself showering down all around, but he doubted it. After another ten minutes searching for Greeley, he gave up after a check of the corral showed the man's huge stallion was gone. He could be most anywhere given a fifteen-minute head start.

Windsor had his men picking up pieces of the body and tossing them into a crate for burial later. He and Snell argued constantly over what had happened. Slocum caught part of the owner's concern that one of his miners had been blown up, but Windsor insisted the entire day shift was accounted for.

Slocum thought the foreman was right. The dead man was likely to be Lester or one of his gang. Since Greeley had disappeared, Slocum had to assume it had been one of Lester's gang rather than the leader himself.

He pushed back the flap of Greeley's huge tent. Inside was dark, but he heard soft movement.

"Sarah Beth?"

"Over here, John. Did you find Lawrence?"

"He left camp, probably to tell Lester that one of his men got careless with some explosive. The blast was too big for regular dynamite. What was your brother thinking, giving his explosive to an outlaw?"

"You've got Lawrence all wrong," Sarah Beth said in a soft voice. "He's not a crook. He just doesn't know who he's dealing with. Are you sure Warren is an outlaw?"

"He's a bank robber and a cold-blooded killer," Slocum said. There was no reason for him to tell her why he was so sure or why he had been studying wanted posters so carefully.

Walking carefully, he made his way across the space between him and Sarah Beth. She was stretched out on a cot. He saw the white oval of her face in the darkness. Slocum lit a lucifer and in the bright flare saw Sarah Beth better. He let the match burn down to his fingers. He dropped the burned stick to the ground.

She had taken off her clothing and stretched out on the cot naked.

"Come to me, John. I need you. I need you so!" Unseen fingers reached for him and pulled him down to the edge of the cot. It tipped as his weight unbalanced it, but he quickly reached out to brace himself. His hand went between her legs. Sarah Beth immediately clamped down with her thighs and held his hand there.

"Why?" he asked.

"Why not?" she said in a hoarse whisper. "Does there have to be more than desire?"

She rubbed herself up and down until his hand pressed into her crotch. He felt wetness from deep inside, and knew how much she wanted him. His own discomfort grew when he hardened and strained against his jeans. She seemed to understand. Her nimble fingers worked on the buttons on his pants and quickly freed him. A warm hand circled him and began working up and down slowly.

Before Slocum could say anything about this, the warm hand was replaced by parted lips and wet tongue moving all over him. She took him into her mouth and slid up and down on his hardness. Slocum sucked in his breath as desire—lust!—spread throughout his loins. He got harder as she worked on him until he ached.

He slid his hand back and forth between her legs, and finally slipped a finger deep into her heated core. Sarah Beth gasped and arched her back. Hips rocking, she began to move around his impaling finger and moan louder.

When she let him slip from her mouth, he knew she was reaching the limits of her passion. Slocum spun around and stood with his legs at the head of the cot, dangling down. She silently kissed him and used her mouth to touch every sensitive spot on his manhood. Bending forward, he thrust his face between her legs. For a moment, she resisted; then her thighs parted for him. His tongue flashed out and delved deeply where his finger had started.

Sarah Beth let out tiny moans of stark pleasure as they continued to arouse each other. Slocum sank down lower and burrowed more, driving himself into her mouth. His hips began moving, slowly at first, and then with increased need. He grabbed the woman's hips to balance himself and pull her in toward his face.

The circuit of pleasure spun back and forth until neither could continue. Slocum felt the rising pressure inside, and then the sudden rush of release. At the same time, he went deaf as Sarah Beth clamped her thighs down on either side of his head. When she relaxed, gasping for air, he moved away and knelt beside the cot. He reached out and ran his forefinger over one of her sleek breasts. He worked up from the base to the tip, still hard with need. She gasped when he caught the rubbery nub between his finger and thumb and began tweaking.

"Oh, John, that was so good—so different. I . . . I'm not used to feeling like this all over."

"Tell your brother he's playing with fire," Slocum said, taking his hand away from her breast. She reached out and caught his wrist and tried to pull him back. He resisted.

"I can't talk to him," she said. "And please, let him be. He'll come around, and we'll all be fine. I promise."

"You don't hold any sway over him," Slocum said. "How did he come to ride with a man like Lester?"

"I'm not sure. They met in some saloon. I wish Lawrence wouldn't get drunk the way he does. He meets such horrid people in saloons and always gets in trouble."

Slocum noticed that her grip on his wrist didn't lessen. She didn't want him to go. He could see her pale, naked body stretched out on the cot, and ideas came to him about what they might do. A tiny twitch down low added to the notion, but Slocum resisted it.

"Was he always like this?"

"He's gotten worse since we came out West. He spends so much time with his chemicals and tests, but now he ignores his experiments and only manufactures his explosive. It's as if he has invented everything there is to invent and is content with that."

"I've heard tell there's not a whole lot more to invent," Slocum said. What more there might be now that there were train tracks crisscrossing the land and telegraph wires ruining the view of the horizon, he couldn't tell. Joe Glidden's barbed wire had spread throughout the country in the ten years since he'd invented it, and had ruined the open range. Slocum wished that could be erased, but he knew it never would.

Why should there be anything more invented? He couldn't see the reason. Moreover, he couldn't see what it would be.

"Lawrence used to go on all the time about what he wanted to do, what he wanted to discover. He doesn't talk like that any longer. Not since he met Mr. Lester."

Slocum pulled away and got free of Sarah Beth's grip, then stood and buttoned himself up.

"You might think on why he changed," Slocum said.

"Don't hurt him, John! I'm begging you!" She swung off the cot and got her arms around his legs, causing him to wobble a mite.

"People are getting blown up using your brother's explosive," he said. "There's a crater out there covered with a man's blood and guts."

"Please, John, don't do this to me. I know what Lawrence does is dangerous. Whoever had that explosive must have stolen it. He wouldn't give it to any of them, even Warren Lester."

"You have a talk with him when he gets back," Slocum said, "but if I find he's knocked you around, I'll make sure he never does it again." He stepped away, then turned his back on her. The darkness of the tent kept her naked beauty from slowing him down. He pushed through the tent flap into the night, and found a different world.

A sharp hint of rain blew down from the higher elevations. He heard Sarah Beth moving behind him, so he walked away from the tent. His thoughts jumbled together and for once, he was not sure what to do. Life usually presented him with easy choices. Mostly, he had to figure out how to stay alive. His Colt Navy helped, but he relied on his instincts. Now those instincts were muddled and confused him even more.

If he had any sense, he would steal a horse and ride the hell out of there. With the marshal over at Sage Junction probably still on the lookout for him, every day he stayed at the Shady Lady Mine was another day he might be recognized and arrested. Mining was dangerous work and accidents happened, but adding some of Greeley's explosive to the dynamite he had used to blow the drainage tunnel for the mine had not been an accident. Someone had tried to kill him.

He suspected it was Lawrence Greeley, but the death of

whoever had been carrying more of the chemist's explosive cast some doubt on that accusation. Slocum stood on the edge of the shallow crater and saw a bright chunk of bone on the far rim. It might be a leg bone or something as large. Greeley might be an arrogant son of a bitch, but he wouldn't be so careless to blow himself up in the middle of the camp. His risk taking took other roads.

Slocum ought to clear out. Warren Lester had a price on his head. If the lawman in Border didn't spot the bank robber, someone out searching for Slocum might. That would bring marshals from all over the area down on the Shady Lady Mine hankering after a five-hundred-dollar reward. Hunting for Lester and finding Slocum would satisfy just about everyone.

Except Slocum.

He had to get out, but he was wary of stealing a horse. That was a crime worse than murder in some places. A man's horse might be all that held death at bay. Then there was Sarah Beth and her dilemma. He knew why she stayed with her brother. She had no other choice. A single woman on her own had few choices when it came to making a living. Slocum couldn't see Sarah Beth with a dozen cowboys in her bed every night. A woman as lovely would have them lined up, all waving money in the air to attract her attention.

What other skills she might have, Slocum didn't know. From the soft skin on her hands, he doubted she had so much as done a wash or scrubbed a floor in her life. Those were things she could learn—but it was better staying with her brother, no matter how he treated her.

Furtive movement caught Slocum's attention. He turned slowly, relying more on hearing than sight. A tiny scraping sound came from the direction of the gold storage vault. Slocum faced the dark, looming building and saw a shadow moving along the side only to disappear around a corner.

His hand went to his six-shooter, but he found only bare hip. His six-gun was still in its holster back in the bunkhouse. The time it would take fetching it might let the skulker get away. If he had proof Lester—or Greeley—wanted to steal Snell's gold, that might go a ways toward earning a reward he could use to buy a horse.

Walking quietly on the rocky ground, he went to the vault and moved to a spot where he could peer around the corner. He caught his breath when he saw how close the man, cloaked entirely in darkness, had come to the trap Slocum had set. One misstep and the blasting caps would detonate the stick of dynamite he had buried.

The mysterious man worked near the spot, but Slocum couldn't tell what he was doing.

Something gave Slocum away. The man jerked upright, uttered a curse, and then lit out. Slocum ran past the small bundle left behind, and was a dozen yards away when an explosion shook the ground. He whirled and heard a shrill cry of pain.

"Don't move, you varmint! You move and I'll blow you clean in two!"

Slocum froze when he saw Snell pointing his shotgun at his middle.

"Slocum! You!"

"You've got this all wrong, Mr. Snell."

"You shut up." Snell shouted, "Windsor, what happened back there?"

"It's Mike. Pyrite Mike Burnside. He blew off his damned leg."

Slocum went cold inside. Another of the miners had detonated his trap. From the hard look on Snell's face, the mine owner knew who had planted the explosive, too.

Slocum raised his hands above his head in surrender.

11

"You move a muscle, Slocum, and I swear, I'll cut you down!" The shotgun in Snell's hands did not waver. "You snake in the grass. You low-down no-account son of a bitch!"

"You've got this all wrong," Slocum said. "I was after somebody trying to blast into the vault to steal your gold."

"So how did Pyrite Mike come to have his leg blowed off? You tried to set a charge and didn't do it right, that's how come. We came on you, you ran, and he got blowed up!"

Slocum started to explain how he had set a trap to protect the gold, then clamped his mouth shut. No matter what he said, it would only make things worse. He looked around to see if he might make a break, but it was wide-open for at least twenty yards. Snell could easily shoot him if he ran. Crossing the distance between him and the mine owner looked like suicide, too. Snell was vigilant and had his dander up. Trying to steal his gold was about the worst thing that could be done to him—Slocum heard that in his voice. Blowing the leg off one of his men wasn't good, but it was nowhere near as criminal as stealing gold from the Shady Lady Mine.

"We got the bleedin' stopped, Boss," Windsor called down. "We're takin' Mike to the bunkhouse."

"And I'll take Slocum to the office. We got some talkin' to do." Snell shoved the shotgun in Slocum's direction and added, "'Less you want me to end it right here and now."

"We'll talk," Slocum said. His mind raced as he tried to figure what the most effective argument would be to get him out of this increasingly hot stew pot. Everything he did tossed another log on the fire.

As he walked past the vault, he saw that the bomb left by the outlaw he had chased off was still in place. Nobody had noticed it. Or had they? Slocum wondered about the miners he had seen on his first shift. They might be working with Lester's gang, or were trying to steal the gold on their own. It wouldn't be that hard for a couple of them to swipe explosives from Lawrence Greeley since the young man was so careless with his invention. Too much swirled around in Slocum's head for him to get any of it straight. All he knew for certain was that hightailing it out of Wyoming was the smartest thing he could do.

"Inside. I don't know how I coulda been so wrong 'bout you, Slocum. I usually see a man's character."

"I wasn't trying to steal your gold," Slocum said. The shotgun never wavered and Snell's attention never faded, even for an instant.

"Set yerse'f down in that chair. The one in the corner. That way you can't make no sudden moves."

Slocum dropped into the chair, his arms pressed into the walls. Snell had it all figured out. The only way to escape was straight ahead out of the chair, and the shotgun made sure he wouldn't do that. Even if he'd had the reflexes of a mountain lion, he would be dead a second before he reached the mine owner.

"I saw somebody behind the vault and went to look," said Slocum. "He ran. That's when you caught me."

"What about the blast that clean cut off Pyrite Mike's leg?"

Slocum hesitated before he lied. Snell was sharp enough to pick up on it.

"So you put the dynamite there, huh? You stole it. You had to. And you were gonna rob me!"

"The man with Lawrence Greeley is the robber. His name's Warren Lester, and he's wanted for bank robbery. You might ask him about plans to rob your gold. He and Greeley could be conniving to do just that."

"Sounds as if you've got an unhealthy acquaintance with the law yerse'f, Slocum."

"I don't deny it, but I wasn't going to rob you."

Snell spat. Before he could say anything more, Windsor came in.

"Not looking good, Boss. Mike's leg had to get cut off another couple inches. We're already up the knee and might have to go above. The blast shredded skin and shattered bone something fierce."

"He'll live, though?"

"Hard to tell. I seen men durin' the war with wounds worse 'n him make it. Then again, I saw soldiers with hardly more than a splinter in their thumb who upped and died. Mike needs a doctor real bad."

"Nearest one's in Sage Junction," Snell said. He caught the way Slocum tensed at the town's name. He squinted a mite and the shotgun stayed centered on Slocum's chest. "You in trouble over there, Slocum? I think the marshal—what's his name?"

"Pritchard," Slocum said, knowing there wasn't a way to wiggle out of this now. "Marshal Pritchard, an old galoot."

"Thas the one. Me and him don't see eye to eye. That's one reason I take my business to Border, though them thieves charge more and are always nasty to me and my boys."

Slocum waited for Windsor to move around in the room. Anything that diverted Snell's attention could be used to help his escape. As if the foreman understood Slocum's intentions, he held back so he didn't get between Snell and his target.

"What are you gonna do with him?" Windsor asked. "Truss him up and take him to Sage Junction?"

"No need for that. Border's got a marshal, more or less." Snell spat accurately into a cuspidor at the side of his desk. "We kin take this varmint in tomorrow mornin'."

Slocum waited for a chance to make a break. Again, Snell was too clever. The old man moved so that he kept Slocum covered when Windsor left. Slocum followed, but Windsor held the door so it couldn't be slammed in Snell's face.

"That old shed on the far side, near the petered-out shaft, is sturdy 'nuff to hold him. You can put a guard on the shack, just to be certain," Snell said.

Slocum heard the shotgun being handed over to Windsor, but again, there wasn't any way he could take advantage of it.

As he and Windsor neared the shed a hundred yards away from the main part of the camp, Slocum said, "If you'd think on it a spell, you'd know I didn't plan to rob Snell."

"I know you didn't. You'd never have got the chance 'cuz me and a couple others are gonna do it."

Slocum started to duck as he realized Windsor was going to gun him down and claim he had tried to run. The crunch of gravel came from far off.

"Oh, Mr. Windsor, excuse me," called Sarah Beth. "I'm hunting for my brother. I think Mr. Slocum saw him earlier."

"You git on outta here, missy," Windsor said.

"That's not a polite way to speak to me, sir!" The woman came over. She saw that Slocum was a prisoner, but made no mention of it.

"Go on, get out of here," Slocum said in a whisper. "He'll kill the both of us."

"I know," she said. Louder to Windsor, she said, "I do believe this is turning into quite a party."

"What do you mean?"

"Four more men? Why, that's almost enough for a square dance. Almost."

Slocum glanced over his shoulder and saw a half dozen miners heading his way.

"Hey, Windsor, the boss told us to come watch over him and make sure nuthin' happens. He's hot to see him go to jail. What'd he do?"

"He blew up Pyrite Mike and tried to steal the gold in the vault," Windsor said.

"Now that is conjecture and nothing more," Sarah Beth said tartly. "If Mr. Slocum is being accused of a crime, he is entitled to his day in court to prove his innocence. Isn't that right?" She addressed the miners directly. "Of course it is. And there's always a lot of free booze at a trial, or so I've heard."

"Not so much over in Border," muttered one. Then the miner brightened and said, "But in Sage Junction, there's likely to be whiskey flowin' like spring runoff." The miners looked happy at the thought of being a part of any trial that would let them drink like fish.

Slocum saw Sarah Beth's tiny smile. She had given them the bait needed to ensure he wouldn't be killed out of hand. Windsor grumbled and made a few choice comments, then stormed off.

"Git on into the prison, Slocum," said a miner. "Ain't never thought of this ramshackle place that way 'fore. That's kinda funny, since we stored hog carcasses in there before."

"There's always something new coming down the pike," Slocum said. He stepped into the shed, and was immediately plunged into intense blackness. The stench of something dead made his nostrils flare. As he poked around, he found a couple meat hooks fastened on the walls. This place had been used as a cold storage locker, and the sturdy walls only looked decrepit on the outside. He slammed his shoulder into one wall and felt it give, but not much, not enough.

"You quit bangin' 'round in there, Slocum. We don't wanna have to hoist you up onto one of them hooks!"

The miners laughed, and then began talking about ways to make him pay for what he'd done to Pyrite Mike. Slocum circled the small room a couple times, hunting for a way out and not finding it. He sat on the floor, disgruntled. More often than not, he was winding up in somebody's lockup. Before, Marshal Pritchard had made it hard to get away, but now he had an entire gold mining camp to escape from.

After he got out of this cell.

The jail in Sage Junction had been simple and impossible to get out of without help. Slocum let his eyes adapt to the low level of light inside, and saw glints of stray light off a meat hook. Slocum worked to pry it loose, and had a vicious weapon after a few seconds of work. He swung it to and fro a few times, listening to the satisfying *swish*. If any of the miners opened the door, they would find sudden death.

Slocum had no desire to hurt any of them. He understood how Snell had jumped to the conclusion he had, but proving his innocence was not going to occur in front of a jury. He took a deep breath and let it out slowly to calm himself from thinking of facing a jury in Sage Junction. With Morgan testifying against him for burning down the Crazy Eights Saloon and killing Allen, he would be strung up before the gavel came down pronouncing him guilty.

Tentatively probing with the metal hook, he worked his way around the walls until he found a spot where the sharp tip sank deeper into the wood. He swung once and caught a chunk of rotting wood with the hook.

"What's that?" A guard outside had heard.

"You're gettin' spooked over nuthin'," said his partner.

"I heard a noise. I'm gonna look around."

"Bring me back some of that whiskey they're swillin' over in the mess hall."

"Go to hell."

The two men argued for a while and then settled down again. Slocum doubted the curious one had made any kind of investigation, but the warning was obvious. He worked as quietly as he could, pulling away hunks of wood until he got a gust of fresh air coming from outside. The scent of rain came through even stronger now. Slocum hoped it would rain. It would cover his tracks when he got away from camp, although there weren't that many directions he could go away from the mine.

As he tore an ever larger hole, he thought on how best to disappear. Stealing a horse was necessary. Maybe one of Greeley's horses would be available. He felt Greeley owed him, though this would hardly be payment enough. Taking Sarah Beth with him was out of the question because she would slow him down, but Slocum knew her life would be a living hell. Her brother would blame her for anything and everything and take out his frustration on her.

"One thing at a time," Slocum muttered as he pulled an entire board free. The wind whistled ominously now through the opening. He worked quietly so the noise wouldn't rouse the guards into actually patrolling around the old shed.

Steal one of Greeley's horses, ride down to the smelter. That was the best way to go. If he rode toward Border, he would find himself caught between a hammer and an anvil. When Snell sent out his men to find Slocum, they would herd him to the town, where he could not expect any reasonable reception. Going to the smelter was a better idea since the river running past it would hide his tracks, provide water, and eventually come out of the maze of canyons somewhere else miles away, giving him real freedom.

The next board pulled free with a screeching of nails ripping through wood. Slocum pushed his head through and caught the wind full in the face. It smelled of freedom. Grunting, he squeezed through and got out, still clutching the meat hook. He didn't need the weapon. The two guards in front of the shed were both sound asleep. Walking softly, he left them and his former prison behind. From the mess hall came boisterous singing and laughter. They were celebrating their victory over a thief, and had forgotten all about how one of their company had been almost killed by Slocum's trap.

He felt a pang of guilt over Pyrite Mike losing his leg, but there wasn't any getting around it. The miner had not been the target, but he had blundered into it. Snell would take care of him. He seemed like that kind of mine owner.

Slocum went to the bunkhouse and peered in. A solitary coal oil lamp burned at the far end, next to Pyrite Mike's bunk. The man slept fitfully, moaning and thrashing about. None of his friends had remained to look after him, preferring to celebrate with a few shots of whiskey. Opening the door slowly kept a gust of wind from waking the man. Slocum slipped in and went directly to his bunk to retrieve his gear.

He went cold inside. His six-shooter and holster were missing. Searching, he ripped back the blanket and patted down the thin pallet and pillow. Everything of his was gone. He cursed under his breath. He wasn't even convicted and already the vultures had snatched all his belongings.

Whoever had taken his Colt Navy would pay for the theft. Knowing it was foolish to be so attached to a firearm, and letting his anger take over anyway, Slocum left the bunkhouse and went to the mess hall to peer through the mud-spattered window hoping to catch sight of the thief. Anyone who had swiped the six-gun would be boasting about it, waving it around, parading like the cock of the walk with the six-shooter shoved into his belt.

If whoever had the six-shooter had strapped it on, he would be even more apparent.

Slocum didn't spot anyone with his pistol.

He moved away from the window and turned, only to plow right into the mine owner. Snell staggered back a step and caught himself. For an instant, the men stared at each other in surprise. Slocum got his wits back first and lifted the meat hook to Snell's throat.

"I don't want to hurt you. I didn't—"

"You won't," came the cold correction from behind him. "Give me the word, Mr. Snell, and I'll add a pound or two of lead to his weight, one bullet at a time."

"I just want to get the hell out of here. I wasn't trying to steal the gold."

"You're a crook," Windsor said, moving around. He held a six-shooter on Slocum. "I might just shoot you, no matter what."

Slocum never had a chance to respond. One instant, he stood with the hook poised at Snell's throat, and the next, he was falling facedown onto the ground, heavy bodies swarming on top of him and pinning him.

"He was tryin' to kill the boss," a miner called. "He cain't git by with that."

"You're right," Windsor said. "String him up. Right over there. The winch'll do for a gallows."

"No, we gotta do this right," protested Snell. Then Slocum heard a crunch and nothing more from the mine owner. Windsor walked around where Slocum could look up. He saw blood on the butt of the six-gun. Windsor had slugged Snell to shut him up.

"I think a necktie party is exactly what we need to set things right. Is Pyrite Mike up to doin' the honors?"

"Aw, Windsor, he's in a coma or whatever you call it. He ain't right in the head yet and might never be, losin' a leg like that and all."

"Then it's up to us to do right by him," Windsor said, stepping back. A cruel smile curled his lips.

"What 'bout Mr. Snell? What happened to him?"

"Slocum here clubbed him, tryin' to gouge out his eyes with that meat hook."

The lie was accepted by the men, who had been drinking so heavily in the mess hall. By now, the entire day shift had poured out. From the sound of boots crunching on gravel, the night shift was joining in. Hurried explanations were made.

Strong hands yanked Slocum to his feet. He faced Windsor and Rourke now. The two foremen had their heads together, arguing. Finally, Windsor backed off and pointed.

"He swings. It's only fittin' after what he did to Mr. Snell. And don't forget Pyrite Mike."

This caused more explanations to be made, until all the miners knew what Slocum had supposedly done. The night shift was as adamant about stretching his neck as the day shift, and they had worked with him long enough to know him better. Only Rourke took Slocum's part, and it quickly became obvious his position fell closer to Snell's than to Windsor's.

"The law oughta decide," Rourke said.

"Shameless Seamus," Windsor said, shaking his head, "I never thought you was a coward. Not till now. Can't you see that *we* are performin' the law's will?"

"Not right. Snell oughta give the go-ahead on this."

"He would, if Slocum hadn't slugged him. He's an old man and might not come around for a spell. Maybe ever. That's a mighty nasty cut he took on his head."

"He did it, Rourke. Windsor slugged Snell. He—" This was as far as Slocum got before a miner wrapped a bandanna around his mouth and tied it tight enough to choke him.

"The winch is a mite bit rusted, but it'll hold his weight."

Slocum was dragged along between two miners, and swung around under the hook a few feet above his head. The device hoisted ore carts on and off the tracks, and moved heavier equipment from one spot in the camp to another. It was strong enough to support him—as long as it took for him to die at the end of a rope.

"Never tied a noose 'fore," complained a miner holding a length of rope. Another snatched it away to show him how it was done. This gave others time to bind Slocum's hands behind his back.

"You think we should put a sack over his head?"

A discussion ensued, and it was finally decided that they wanted to see Slocum's face as he died.

He was pushed and shoved into place and, amid great cheers, had the noose dropped over his head and cinched up around his neck. More argument raged about the proper slack to leave in it.

"Don't matter much if we break his neck or he chokes to death, now does it?" asked Windsor.

Slocum locked eyes with the foreman. Windsor was enjoying this for reasons only Slocum knew.

"Let's hoist the son of a bitch, men!"

A ratchet began making *clank-clank* sounds as the rope tightened around Slocum's neck.

12

The rope tightened and forced Slocum onto tiptoe to keep from choking. Another second and he would leave the earth—for good.

Just as he was sure he was a goner, he felt the ground quiver beneath his toes, and then a tremendous explosion rocked the mining camp. He swung back and tried not to lose his balance and hang himself. Somewhere behind him, he heard the rusty wheels turning, and he feared the miner working the winch would keep cranking until he had finished his chore.

He blinked through tears caused by the cloud of dust that had rolled over the mining camp, and saw indistinct figures running this way and that, all shouting and some bellowing that they had been hurt. He had no idea what had happened.

And then it didn't matter. The rope slackened around his neck, and he fell to his knees. The hook that had held the rope banged into the back of his head, knocking him forward. He struggled to get up, but with his hands bound behind him, he had a time of it.

"Don't wiggle around so, John," came Sarah Beth's urgent command. A sudden pressure on his wrists was followed by release. She had cut his bonds. He rubbed his wrists and got to his feet.

"What happened?"

"Here," she said, shoving his Colt and holster into his hands. "We've got to get out of here right now."

"You took my gun?"

"Right after they locked you up. I thought I'd use it to get you free, but when I got to the shed you had already escaped. I tried to catch up, but by then Windsor had worked the miners up into a lynch mob."

Slocum ran his fingers over the welt around his neck where the rope had cut in. He wasn't likely to forget Windsor's part in trying to lynch him.

"You set off the blast?"

"It was the only thing I could think to do. I used the explosive that had been stacked next to the gold vault. There was an awful lot of it, more than enough to blow the building into splinters. Whoever placed the charge didn't know how powerful the explosion would be."

"It was Windsor," Slocum said. "He and a couple other miners were going to blow up the vault and steal the gold."

"I heard one of them got a leg blown off."

"I set the trap for them, but it didn't work the way I had hoped. A miner named Pyrite Mike stomped on it."

"Him? I know him! He's one of Windsor's men," Sarah Beth said. "I've seen him and another man talking together."

Slocum mulled this over. The two miners he had spotted digging at the side of the vault had to work in the day shift—they were Windsor's henchmen. He felt a mite better thinking that Pyrite Mike had been one of his intended victims all along. Not only had Pyrite Mike been one of those who were trying to steal the gold, he was probably one of those who had gunned down Rick.

"How do we get out of here?" Slocum asked.

"I've saddled a horse for you. It's one of Lawrence's, but he won't miss it. I can always say it ran off in the confusion, if he mentions it."

"Come with me," Slocum said, grabbing her arm. Sarah Beth turned a dirt-streaked, frightened face to him and shook her head.

"I can't. I have to wait for Lawrence to return."

"You don't belong with him." Slocum saw her waiting for him to say something more—but he couldn't bring himself to say it. Those words would have pushed her off the fence, but would have also burdened him with taking care of her beyond simple escape.

"I'll lie if they ask where you went," she said. "The miners are sure to notice a horse is missing, unless you take all of them. Then they wouldn't know for sure if there are horses going in every which direction."

Slocum had planned to do that very thing, but for a different reason. He didn't want any of the miners mounting up to come after him. Snell's mules were hardly a match for a horse when it came to speed.

"There's the horse, John. Please, be careful." Sarah Beth turned her dirt-streaked face upward and her eyes closed. He gave her a quick, unsatisfying kiss. If it had been more, she would have come with him. Slocum knew she was not safe with a brother who beat her up, but she was better off with Greeley than on the lam beside him on the trail.

He swung into the saddle and saw it was his own. She had taken all his gear from the bunkhouse. He twisted around and checked to be sure these were his saddlebags. They were. He had a spare pistol there, along with ample ammunition if he got into a prolonged gunfight. If he rode fast and hard, he wouldn't have any pursuit worth mentioning.

From the camp came angry cries. They had discovered the blast was a diversion for him to get away from their hanging.

"Be careful," Slocum told her. "Don't let them bully you. Don't let anybody bully you." With that, he snapped the reins and took off like a rocket on the gelding, making his way out of camp toward the road heading down toward

Border. Before he had ridden a couple hundred yards, he heard the thunder of hooves behind him. Sarah Beth had released the rest of Greeley's remuda.

He waited for the spooked horses to gallop past on the road to Border, then cut off at an angle, circled the camp, and found the double-rutted road that was leading toward the smelter down below in the next valley. The sun was just poking up over the peak to the east, letting him ride faster than he had expected. Behind in the camp, he still heard angry shouts and orders being barked by both Windsor and Rourke.

Slocum hoped Snell was all right, but if Windsor had anything to do with it, the mine owner might end up dead. If that happened, Slocum knew he would have another death chalked up against him. He had killed plenty of men in his day, but the two here in western Wyoming—Stanford Allen and Rick—were not his doing.

As he rode, he wondered about the fire and subsequent death of the Crazy Eights' owner. Whatever trouble Slocum had stumbled onto at the Shady Lady Mine, the trouble in Sage Junction had been separate. Lady luck had turned into quite a whore for him. He had left Denver fast and had fallen into an even worse cauldron of death and explosions.

An hour of riding brought him to the valley floor. To the north lay the smelter. Curls of black smoke already spiraled into the sky, telling him they were reducing another load of ore from the mine and turning it into gold bars. He felt Snell owed him something for his trouble, but going to the smelter and adding one or two of those shiny metal ingots to his saddlebags was not going to help him any. He knew guards at the smelter watched every speck of gold that was melted out of the ore, and only stopped watching when it was freighted up the steep slope and back to the mine, where it went into the supposedly secure vault.

Slocum knew Greeley's explosive was more than enough to blast open a regular vault. What lay inside the wooden walled building was a question he'd like to answer, but in spite of it not being as strong as a bank vault, he would get no chance to find out. Snell stored the gold until a monthly shipment into Salt Lake City emptied the vault so it could start to be filled again.

He had no idea how much gold was transferred in every shipment, but from what he had seen of the rich veins and the visible gold in the ore, it could amount to thousands of dollars a month. The Shady Lady Mine was very profitable for Snell and any partners he had.

The lure of doing what they had accused him of attempting appealed more and more to Slocum as he rode, but by noonday, he drew rein and came back to the here and now. Somewhere down the canyon, along the river, he heard men joshing one another. The sound of their horses told him at least a half dozen riders were ahead of him.

He left the river and melted into the forest to ride another quarter mile before he heard the men again. This time, he dismounted and advanced on foot to see who was making so much noise. Four men splashed around in the river, their union suits bright red in the daylight. Finding a spot to watch, Slocum studied not the bathing men, but the rocks on either side of the river.

The water narrowed here and rushed over hidden rocks to kick up froth and foam before widening once more. At the narrows sat a man with a rifle resting in the crook of his left arm. This sentry was alert and watched the forested area on the far side of the river. Slocum moved a bit and found another guard on the near bank giving his side a similar once over. He wasn't as attentive, allowing Slocum a chance to hunker down without being seen.

"Git yer bony asses out of the water. We got territory to cover 'fore sundown."

"Ah, stuff it," called back a man in the river. "Marshal Pritchard got a bug up his ass over that Slocum fella. We ain't gonna find him after all this time. He's prob'ly in Canada by now."

"I say he headed south to Mexico," said another. "That's

where I'd go, them purty señoritas and all the *cerveza* you kin drink."

"Beer? You'd go to Mexico and drink beer? Tequila. Drink the real stuff. It'd put hair on your chest."

The men argued over which way Slocum had headed, giving him the chance to slip back into the woods and return to his horse. He might sneak past them, but he wasn't sure what he would find farther up the canyon. If the Sage Junction marshal had a camp there, more of his posse might be waiting for the return of these six. Slocum would find himself in a world of hurt and never be able to shoot his way free if he trapped himself between two groups of lawmen.

He turned back in the direction he had just come and headed for the smelter. Once past it, he could go north and be in Canada in a week or two. He realized this was the direction he should have gone since Sage Junction lay to the south and nobody was hunting for him to the north. Or so he hoped. Even if they were, he had a good chance of losing them in the Grand Tetons.

He set a quicker pace, and reached the smelter just at sundown, but found himself faced with another problem. A gold shipment was being readied for transport up to the camp. Snell—or Windsor—had sent a dozen miners to guard it, and they all milled around, making it impossible for him to slip past.

"Do it in the morning," a freighter said. "Ain't no way I'm goin' up that road in the dark."

Slocum caught parts of the argument. The guards wanted the driver to attempt the trip so they could return to camp, but he steadfastly refused. The freighter showed great common sense, but when Slocum heard what the man's victory meant, he wished he had been a lot more daring.

"Spread out and make sure nobody's movin' 'round in the valley tonight. I don't want bandits flankin' us 'fore dawn," the driver said. "Don't leave any stone unturned out there. Outlaws might just be hidin', waitin' fer the gold to get loaded so they can steal it."

A lengthy argument ensued. Finally, the guards grumbled but obeyed. Slocum found himself caught between the mine guards to his north and the marshal's posse behind him.

He shook his head in wonder at his bad luck. He might camp for the night, but the chance of being found increased with every passing minute. The guards were pissed and willing to take it out on anyone they found. It wasn't possible they would not recognize him since they were all from the Shady Lady.

Being caught between the jaws of a vise, Slocum could not go north or south or stay where he was. That left only one direction. He turned his gelding up the steep road and headed back to the mining camp up in the mountains. His luck had to change for the better. With so many miners guarding the shipment, that meant smaller crews and exhausted men after their shift ended. Riding on through the camp to the road leading to Border was his only hope of getting away from the law and Snell's men.

As he rode into camp just after the night shift went into the mines, Slocum thought he heard Snell calling out orders to Rourke. Relief flooded Slocum as he realized that the mine owner was still alive and that Windsor hadn't killed him. Skirting the main yard, Slocum rode toward Greeley's tent. Light spilled out the open flap, but he didn't see or hear anyone moving inside. The temptation to see if Sarah Beth was waiting there was great, but Slocum overcame it.

What he could not overcome, though, was curiosity at a dark form moving from the bunkhouse toward the gold vault. Whoever it was moved silently and took pains not to be seen, darting from shadow to shadow. The waning moon wouldn't rise for another hour, so Slocum saw only movement and not detail.

He damned himself for being suicidal, but he had to identify who it was moving toward the gold storage building. He knew the last shipment of the month was still downhill at the smelter and wouldn't be sent up until morning. If the load was heavy enough, it could take all day for the wagon to arrive, for the gold to be stored the next night.

If his guess was right, the gold would be kept here only one night, and transported to Salt Lake City the following morning. That meant increased security tomorrow night, but less tonight, making this the best time to plant more explosives. How the theft was supposed to happen was something of a mystery to Slocum. Stealing it on the way to Salt Lake City seemed a better idea than blowing up the vault and trying to escape with heavy gold bars, but Windsor and his men—or was it Lester and Greeley?—had something in mind.

He wanted to find out what it was.

He put his horse in Greeley's corral, where it tossed its head and snorted, being home again. Slocum took a few minutes to feed and water the horse. When he rode again, he'd have to travel hard and fast. Having the horse in the best condition possible might mean the difference between a rope taut around his neck and keeping his freedom.

Backtracking, he went to the road leading to the smelter. From there, he had a good view of the gold vault. Heavy shadows masked whatever the man was doing at the side of the building, but he worked diligently. Slocum drew his six-shooter and advanced slowly, walking as quietly as any Apache brave on a hunt. He froze when he lost sight of the man at the side of the building.

Dropping to his belly, he waited to see if the man showed himself again. After a few minutes and not seeing anything, Slocum stood. The explosion lifted him off his feet and tossed him ten feet back. His heels caught in the dirt and sent him sliding away.

The building caught fire and burned, but only for a few seconds. The quickness of the fire dying drew Slocum forward, in spite of the rush of miners from the bunkhouse and mess hall.

He slipped his six-gun back into the holster and pulled down the brim of his hat. If there was enough confusion, he wouldn't be noticed.

Slocum knew he should hightail it, but he went instead to the vault. The building's side had been blown away, and the steel wall of the vault itself had been peeled away like removing the rind of an orange.

From the fitful fires burning in the aftermath of the blast, he saw the shelves in the vault.

They were bare of gold.

13

Slocum stepped over the debris left by the explosion and poked through the vault a few seconds, then backed out. Shouts coming from all over warned him the miners were coming to see what had happened. Knowing he had only seconds, Slocum pulled down his hat to hide his face, although this wasn't much of a disguise. He melted into the cloud of dust slowly drifting from the building. The powerful odor choked him—and he knew what had been used to open the vault like an airtight can of tomatoes.

Lawrence Greeley's explosive produced a powerful blast and a distinctive lingering odor after it detonated.

"What happened? Oh, my God, the gold's all missing!"

Slocum kept walking, angling to take advantage of the mess hall to hide him. He leaned against the building, head down, as three miners raced past him.

"Heard it was the dynamite shed what blowed up," one said.

"Couldn't be. It'd still be poppin'. It had to be the gold. Somebody's done stole all the gold we mined over the last month."

Slocum took it all in and wondered at the blast. Nobody

could have stolen the gold so quickly. That meant the shelves in the vault were empty before the explosion. He peered around the corner of the mess hall in time to see Snell and Windsor arguing again. The mine owner waved his arms about like a windmill spinning in a tornado. Windsor looked perturbed, too, making Slocum think the foreman hadn't been the one to empty the vault.

A considerable amount of gold was on its way upslope from the smelter, but how much had been poured into bars and stored over the past three weeks? Slocum suspected he would be happy to spend even a small portion of that gold.

He ducked back when he heard Snell shout, "Slocum! It's got to be that snake in the grass! Who else'd steal my gold?"

"He tried before," Windsor pointed out. This set off a new round of denunciations from all the gathered miners, most of them pointing out the gold would still be on the shelves if they had actually strung up their prisoner when they had the chance.

Slocum touched the raw welt on his neck where the noose had cut into his flesh. Who would they have blamed if they'd gone ahead and dangled him from the winch? His nostrils flared in disgust. Windsor would still blame him, making the accusation that the gold had been taken and hidden before the hanging.

Windsor and Pyrite Mike were a couple of miners who had tried to steal the gold. Who *had* spirited it away? And how had they done it without anyone noticing?

Slocum had more questions than answers. He walked from the camp without being noticed. The uproar at the gold vault would render him invisible for a while yet, if he didn't do anything to draw attention to himself. Once mounted, he rode past Greeley's tent and saw that it was deserted. Greeley had taken his belongings, but left the huge tent behind. All the horses in the crude corral were gone, too, telling him nobody had tried to round them up after Sarah Beth had released them the day before as a diversion. The young chemist had left without returning, giving Slocum an idea who had stolen the gold.

How it had been done so slickly and without blowing open the vault was a question he'd have to answer later. The uproar in the mining camp was settling down and the men were prowling about, hunting for clues. Slocum rode around a curve in the road, shielding him from direct view. Pursuing him would be a chore since all they had were mules, but Marshal Pritchard's posse down in the valley was mounted. All the head start he had was the time it would take the lawmen to ride from the valley to the Shady Lady Mine.

Making his way down the mountainside proved easier than he expected, possibly because the prospect of having a noose around his neck once more lent speed to his travel. Every time the gelding tried to slow, Slocum used his spurs to keep moving. Varying the gait rested the horse a mite, and then taxed it to the fullest. By the time he reached the bottom of the road, he came to the fork with one side going to Border and the other northward. Slocum never hesitated turning his horse's face toward the north. He wanted to be out of the territory as fast as he could.

Only a mile along the road, he saw wagon tracks in the soft shoulder. Slocum dismounted and knelt to study the tracks. From the wobble in a rear wheel, he decided the wagon was heading in the same direction he was. He mopped his forehead with his dirty bandanna and considered leaving the road and cutting across country. He didn't want to overtake a bunch of settlers and have them tell a pursuing posse when he had ridden past.

On the other hand, the country was rugged here. The Tetons rose to the northeast, and the range to his west was more than foothills. The road had been cut here for a reason. It was about the only way through the countryside that didn't require a considerable amount of blasting to clear the way.

"Blasting," he muttered. Slocum examined the wagon tracks again. He measured the width and decided this wasn't likely a wagon driven by the settlers. Their wheels were set wider. This was more like the wagon Lawrence Greeley used to carry his equipment.

Slocum took a deep breath and held it while he thought on the matter. He wanted nothing to do with Greeley or his powerful explosives, but seeing Sarah Beth again had to be balanced against that. Then there was the matter of Snell's missing gold. Windsor and his henchmen hadn't stolen it. Seeing the foreman's expression when he laid eyes on the empty shelves in the vault was more eloquent than any denial. If it wasn't Windsor, it had to be either Greeley or Warren Lester.

If Greeley and Lester had partnered up, the wagon might carry a fair amount of stolen gold. Slocum wasn't a greedy man, but the notion of a couple gold bars weighing down his saddlebags was mighty appealing. Let Greeley and Lester keep most of their stolen gold. He deserved some compensation for all the trouble he had gone through.

He touched the welt on his neck and winced. The pain was more than physical. His brush with getting his neck stretched had left him wanting revenge on those responsible. Blaming the miners and even Snell wasn't possible, since Windsor had been the one goading them to hang Slocum. That would cover Windsor's tracks when he stole the gold.

But the gold was gone. Windsor would have watched an innocent man strung up for nothing.

"Follow or forget the whole damned thing?" The horse didn't respond, even with a toss of his head. All the gelding did was stare straight ahead, as if wanting nothing to do with any harebrained scheme Slocum might cook up.

"I'm flat broke," Slocum went on as he turned the facts over and over in his mind, examining them from all directions. When he came to a conclusion, he hoped it was based on solid logic and not on wanting to see Sarah Beth once more. She was being held a prisoner by her brother. Slocum was not inclined to come riding to her aid, but he might convince her to show some backbone and stand up to

Greeley, even if it meant sneaking out in the dead of night and never looking back.

He mounted and rode with his attention fixed on the road ahead for the first sign of Greeley's wagon. The tracks didn't tell him if Lester or anyone else rode alongside, but just because he didn't see them didn't mean they weren't there. He could search the broad area on either side of the road, but time wore down on him, like the pages of a book pressing a flower.

The wagon tracks veered from the road and headed west, forcing Slocum to make a decision. He could ride on and forget everything that had happened in Wyoming. He was flat broke, but could always find a job somewhere farther north tending cattle or working again in a saloon. Living off the land was easy enough with the profusion of game all around him. He could do that.

He turned his horse to follow the wagon tracks.

Slocum went for his six-shooter when he saw the wagon ahead in a stand of junipers. The team had been corralled some distance away, but the sound of his approach was hidden by the rushing of a large stream not far off.

Nowhere did he see anyone. While they might be lying in wait for him, he doubted an ambush was all that likely. He would have seen a flurry of motion, and their horses would have been spooked just enough to draw attention to the trap. He rode up directly and looked around. The wagon had been partly unloaded, but most of Greeley's equipment remained in crates. A small cooking fire had been laid out in the direction of the stream, but had not been lit. Food piled around a nearby log was already drawing insects. Before long, wolves or bears would come for it unless it was cooked soon.

A twig breaking spun him around in the saddle. He aimed his six-shooter directly at Sarah Beth as she came from the depths of the woods, holding up her skirt to keep a pile of blackberries from tumbling out. It took her several seconds to realize she wasn't alone. Her blue eyes widened when she saw the six-gun pointed straight at her.

"John, don't shoot."

"Where are the others? Your brother? His assistants?" He hesitated, then asked the real question. "Is Lester around?"

"No, no, they're all gone. All of them." She advanced hesitantly, as if not sure whether he would gun her down or let her live. Seeing this, Slocum holstered his Colt Navy and stepped down from the horse.

"I saw the wagon tracks in the road. When did you clear out of the mining camp?"

"Right after I helped you. I knew there wasn't any way I could stay there. They'd suspect me right away. Me or Lawrence."

"As if your brother would piss on me if I were on fire," Slocum said.

"You don't know him, John. He's not as bad as you think."

Slocum reached out and laid his hand on her cheek. Sarah Beth flinched away.

"Still sore from when he hit you?"

"He's upset right now. There's so much going wrong in his life. He . . . he needs to work it all out." She looked up imploringly at him. "I need your help, John."

He went cold inside. He knew what she was going to ask, and he didn't want to repay her for saving him from the hangman's noose. But what choice did he have?

"What's happened to him?"

"He and that awful Warren Lester have gone off to rob a stagecoach."

"What?" This made no sense to Slocum if either Greeley or Lester had stolen the gold from the mine.

"Lester heard there was a payroll aboard the stage coming down from Montpelier. I think it is going to Sage Junction. Lester wanted to rob the stage, and Lawrence didn't argue about it. If anything, he . . ." Her words trailed off.

"He encouraged Lester," Slocum finished for her. She nodded mutely. "Did they steal the gold from the mine?"

"What? The gold's gone? I don't understand."

"Somebody used a passel of your brother's explosive to blow a hole in the side of the vault, but there wasn't anything inside."

"No gold? Where'd it go?"

"That's a poser," Slocum admitted. None of the people he suspected of stealing Snell's gold were acting as if they had become suddenly rich. Windsor was angry at finding the gold gone—he wasn't able to steal it. If Lester or Greeley had the gold, they would be bragging about it, not plotting to rob a stage with a paltry amount of money being shipped. Slocum doubted Sarah Beth when she said it was a payroll. More likely, one bank was sending currency to another. Sage Junction needed a fair amount of money on hand to deal with the miners when they came to town, that being the closest place they were likely to be welcomed since Border pretty much rolled up the streets at sundown.

"I don't care about that," she said with growing urgency in her voice. "I don't want Lawrence hurt. He doesn't know a thing about holding up stages or being an outlaw."

"He's got a good teacher," Slocum said. "The poster I saw on Lester said he was as likely to kill everyone on the stagecoach as rob them."

"Lawrence isn't sure what he wants. He's such a young man, and he's always been so bright. It hasn't been easy for Lawrence, ever. He didn't fit in anywhere, and we came out West to find a place to settle down."

"He's not going about it the right way if he's taken to robbing stages," Slocum said.

"Bring him back to me, John. I'll take care of him as I always have."

He rolled over the problems facing him. Then Sarah Beth played her trump card, which decided him.

"You owe me your life. I hate saying this, but your debt to me will be repaid when you bring Lawrence back safe and sound."

Slocum could have ridden due west across some mighty rough country and been lost within a day. He wouldn't have such worries confronting him. But she was right. He did owe her. He stepped up into the saddle and rode, hoping to find Lawrence Greeley before he got himself killed.

He reached the road, and knew he had to keep riding north. Lester and his gang were experienced road agents, and would find the best spot to hold up the stage. Why the outlaw let Greeley ride with him wasn't something Slocum wanted to think on too hard. As soon as the young chemist had outlived his usefulness, Lester would plug him and ride off without so much as a look back.

Yet another question that didn't have much of an answer was what Lester needed Greeley for at all.

He had ridden for only a half hour when he heard a distant boom that was all too familiar now. A large explosives charge had been detonated. Slocum put his heels to his gelding and galloped ahead, knowing he might be riding into a trap and not much caring now. He had gotten madder and madder at himself for agreeing to rescue Sarah Beth's worthless brother. Greeley might be the best chemist in the whole damned country, but rescuing him from himself was a fool's errand.

Slocum spotted a rising cloud of white smoke ahead. He slowed his headlong pace and trotted the gelding around a bend in the road. Slocum read the makings of an expert ambush. The road took a sharp bend here, forcing the driver to slow to negotiate the rocks. As the stagecoach slowed, outlaws on either side of the road had shown themselves. It was as if Slocum saw it all being reenacted before his eyes.

Then the outlaws opened fire and killed the driver for no good reason. Slocum saw the shotgun still in the driver's box. From the position of the man's body sprawled over the side, he had stopped, lashed his reins around the brake, and stood, hands in the air. Lester had opened up and cut him down.

Two passengers had either boiled out of the compartment, eager to fight, or they had been forced out and similarly gunned down. Three men dead in the span of a few seconds.

Slocum circled the stage with its nervous team and found the strongbox—or what remained of it. Too much explosive had been used to blow off the lock. Bits of the metal strongbox had flown in all directions like a land mine detonating. Slocum wondered if any of the outlaws had been injured. He scouted for blood, but couldn't find any. Dropping to the ground, he led his horse to the sundered box and kicked at it with his toe.

The lid hung by a single hinge. Slocum's kick dislodged it to reveal an empty box. If there had been scrip inside, it had burned from the explosion. The amount of soot he saw smeared inside the box didn't give him any clue whether the money had been taken or burned. When the explosive went off, it not only created a monumental shock wave that tore the box apart, it also generated heat intense enough to melt steel.

He walked around the area for a half hour, trying to figure out where the outlaws had hidden, where they had ridden in from, and what direction they had taken leaving. The rocky terrain prevented him from getting a good idea about any of this. All he knew was that Lester and his gang hadn't ridden past him when he had approached the scene of the robbery.

It seemed unlikely Lester had ridden back along the road north toward Montpelier, unless he wanted to go farther into Idaho and escape the law. Slocum wasn't sure who would be responsible for catching a robber stealing money from Idaho but committing the crime in Wyoming. No country sheriff would take responsibility. This was beyond the jurisdiction of a town marshal. Federal marshals and deputies might be interested. More likely, the stage company would hire private detectives to go after the gang responsible for killing two passengers and a driver. That was bad publicity for them, and would hurt the company more than the loss of a few dollars in paper money.

Slocum found what might be the outlaws' trail heading eastward into the Wyoming mountains. At this point, the

Grand Tetons poked into the sky to the northeast, but the closest hills were more likely part of another, lesser mountain chain. Names didn't matter. Finding the outlaws did.

He rode, expecting to find another body along the trail. Lester had no use for Greeley anymore, unless he wanted the chemist to make more of the potent explosive. Lester had shown he had no idea how to use it by demolishing both the strongbox and its contents. All the robbery had netted the road agents was whatever they had taken off the three dead men.

From the way the victims were dressed, Slocum doubted Lester had gotten rich off this robbery.

After riding for an hour on what he thought was the trail, Slocum had to admit defeat. The rocky ground hid tracks too well. The road agents could have veered off the trail at any point, and he would never have been able to tell. Lester was a wily crook, and had to know that if a posse came after him, concealing his trail now meant he had all the time in the world to make his getaway.

If he even wanted to go anywhere else. Slocum took off his hat, wiped his forehead, and looked ahead into the maze of rock. Warren Lester could find a hideout in any of those branching, winding, steep-walled canyons. Not even sure he was on the right trail, Slocum could hunt fruitlessly for weeks. Or he could ride into an ambush and be dead before he hit the ground.

Since he had not seen Lawrence Greeley's carcass drawing buzzards along the trail, he figured the chemist still rode with Lester. Whether he went willingly or was a prisoner, Slocum had no way of knowing without actually finding him and the outlaw band.

Slocum had to come up with a different way of searching out Lawrence Greeley. He turned his horse about and rode from the mountainous region.

14

Slocum rode back to where he had left Sarah Beth with her wagon. It didn't surprise him to find the wagon abandoned and the team gone. Her brother must have returned and taken her, along with the horses. A few minutes of searching for spoor revealed a set of hoofprints that could have been caused by as many as a half dozen horses. Greeley, along with Lester and his gang, had come here by some back trail Slocum had not seen.

This was a chance for him to ride away and never look back. Then he knew he could never do it, not because of Sarah Beth and her slavish devotion to her brother, but because of the dead men piling up all around. Allen had died, Rick had been gunned down, three men at the stagecoach had died—how many more were slated to be snuffed out? Except for the miner, all the killing had been done in a deadly circle around Lawrence Greeley.

Whether he had fallen in with bad company or somehow caused it all himself, the killing had to stop. It wasn't Slocum's job, but he felt responsible.

He followed the tracks for a mile, and then lost them in a wide, shallow stream. Hunting for another hour or two might not show where Greeley, Lester, and Sarah Beth had gone. Slocum decided it was time to put his own scheme into play, as dangerous as it was.

He put his heels to his horse and headed southward, toward Sage Junction and what might be the dumbest stunt he had ever pulled. As he rode, he worked over his plan. Marshal Pritchard was an old man and couldn't get around the way he once did. Slocum hoped that meant he would stay close to his office and not go prowling around town too much. All Slocum needed was a few minutes' discussion with a single man in Sage Junction. Then he could be on his way.

One man. Slocum knew he was chasing smoke, but he wanted to try, even if it meant being recognized. He rode slowly, took his time to cover his tracks, and by nightfall the next day he was ready to ride into Sage Junction. The town had not changed much. The burned smell from the Crazy Eights Saloon still hung in the air, possibly because people had pawed through the ruins hunting for anything they could salvage. This kicked up soot, and even exposed a few hot spots that still smoldered. If Slocum had been the fire chief, he would have seen that the fire was entirely drenched, but that required extra effort.

The saloon was gone and no use to anyone, so why fool with it any longer? Slocum could almost hear the volunteer firemen saying that.

Cloaked in twilight, he rode down the middle of the main street, not looking around, trying not to draw attention. He rode a different horse and wore a new shirt. A few citizens called to him and waved. He acknowledged their greeting without turning. He simply touched the brim of his battered Stetson, making certain to hide his face with his hand as he did so.

He remembered where the town pharmacist had his apothecary, and rode around to the rear of the store. A single lamp burned inside to hold back the night. The pharmacist undoubtedly worked late to mix up the medicines needed by the townsfolk. Or perhaps he had another order to fill. If Lawrence Greeley needed chemicals to mix up more of his powerful explosive, the apothecary might carry them. If not, the pharmacist had connections to order whatever Greeley might need.

Slocum rapped lightly on the rear door. No answer. He lifted the latch and pushed on the creaking wood, but the door refused to budge. Putting his shoulder to it, he heard something move inside along the floor. When the door popped open suddenly, Slocum lost his balance and went to his hands and knees. Less than a foot away he saw the reason the door had been blocked. A man sprawled on his back, sightless eyes peering up at the ceiling.

A bullet had robbed the pharmacist's life and caused a small red splotch to spread on his white apron. Slocum hastily climbed to his feet and closed the door behind him. He pressed against one wall when a man and a woman passed along the boardwalk in front of the apothecary and peered in the window. His breath gusted out when they walked on, never realizing the town pharmacist had been killed with a single shot through the heart.

Edging forward, Slocum pulled down the blinds before looking around the small shop. He didn't have to have an inventory to know where items had been stolen. Those shelves were in disarray, while others above and below were in perfect order. He tried to guess what chemicals had been taken, but couldn't. It took no imagination at all to know those were the chemicals Lawrence Greeley needed to make more of his potent explosive.

Slocum settled down behind the pharmacist's desk and opened a ledger. He ran his finger down one column after another until he found the notation he wanted. Greeley had placed an order several weeks earlier, but Slocum couldn't figure out if Greeley had picked it up or if the chemicals had ever arrived. All the pharmacist had noted was the company in Salt Lake City where he had placed the order.

"Hey, Ulrich, you ready?" Somebody rattled the front

door. Slocum's hand flashed for his six-shooter, but he did not draw. "We been waitin' for you almost an hour. You got no cause to work all the time, not when there's a new whore over at the saloon just waitin' for us. Ulrich? You all right, Ully?"

Slocum walked on cat's feet to the rear door, and pulled it shut behind him as the front door exploded inward. He caught a glimpse of a burly man with a florid face, and then was mounted and riding from town. Slocum had barely reached the end of the block when Ulrich's friend sounded the alarm that his friend had been murdered.

If he stayed in Sage Junction a minute longer, somebody would spot him. Slocum knew who would be blamed for the murder then. Everywhere he went—when he followed Greeley's trail—he had to step over one dead body after another.

He rode west out of town and found the main road curling toward Salt Lake City. Whatever supplies the town got were freighted in from the larger city. Making sense out of the pharmacist's crabbed handwriting had been difficult, but Slocum thought another shipment was due either tomorrow or the next day. Most of the supplies wouldn't be of any interest to Greeley, but if he hadn't gotten what he needed from Ulrich, it would be on the supply wagon.

What happened to cause the pharmacist's murder was known only to the killer now, but Slocum didn't have to work too hard to find some likely reasons. Ulrich realized what Greeley was doing with the chemicals, had refused to sell any more, and was killed for being a good citizen. Or Ulrich might have wanted a cut, so Greeley—or Lester— had shot him to keep the pharmacist quiet. Greeley might have turned furious with Ulrich when he didn't have the right chemicals. From what Slocum had seen, Greeley wasn't very good at controlling his temper.

Slocum ground his teeth together as he remembered how Greeley had slapped Sarah Beth back at the mining camp. If the chemist had tasted the power that violence afforded, he might be running unchecked now. Sarah Beth had held him down, soothed him, told him everything was all right and that he was a damned genius. Greeley had probably taken that to heart, and ignored the rest of her attempts at civilizing him.

Two hours' ride into the night tuckered Slocum out, and caused his gelding to wobble as he walked. Slocum decided to camp for the night, and hunt for the best spot along the road to intercept a supply wagon from Salt Lake City in the morning. He wasn't sure what he would do since the driver wasn't likely to know what any of his cargo was, but the man had to know what portion of the load had been bought by Ulrich.

All Slocum needed to do was look it over and decide if he should take it from the freighter to use as bait, or if he should let the wagon roll on and then watch what happened.

He slept fitfully, woke before dawn, and boiled enough coffee to keep him alert. His larder was running empty and all he had, other than the potent coffee, was a moldy hunk of venison jerky. He needed to hunt to find something more if he intended to wait even a long as a week for the supply wagon.

Slocum rode on, following the meandering road through foothills, and finally out onto a stretch where he could see a couple miles of road.

"Son of a bitch." He took off his hat and slapped it against his thigh. His idea of waiting for the supply wagon was a good one. Unfortunately, someone else had had the same idea. The wagon was tipped on its side where it had run off the road.

Slocum trotted the half mile to where the wagon balanced on one side, its wheels slowly turning in the morning breeze. The contents had been spilled out, but they weren't strewn in a haphazard fashion as if they had been thrown clear. Some boxes had been ripped open and the contents pawed through. Other crates were stacked neatly. Different men had searched through the cargo.

Dropping from his horse, Slocum approached, and saw the freighter pinned under the wagon. He must have whipped his team to top speed, veered off the road into a ditch, and flipped over. The only reason a grizzled old freighter such as this one would put on such speed was to evade pursuit.

Slocum found hoofprints of three or four horses, and re-lived the freighter's last minutes of life. Road agents appeared on either side of the wagon. The driver tried to get away, and paid for it with his life. There might have been gunshots, but Slocum doubted it. The freighter's body wasn't even cold to the touch, so the wreck had happened only a short while earlier. If there had been gunfire, Slocum would likely have heard it.

He kicked over boxes and hunted for something he could use. A case of canned peaches had already been rifled, leaving only two cans. Slocum took those. The rest of the cargo consisted of yard goods, nails, and medical supplies. Whoever had stolen the rest of the peaches had ignored the medicine, but had taken something more.

Slocum looked for a shipping manifest, but didn't find it. The missing cargo must have been destined for Ulrich's shelves—and consisted of the chemicals Greeley needed. Nothing else made sense. If another gang of outlaws had robbed this shipment, there wouldn't be any food left at all, and more likely, they would have righted the wagon and stolen it, too. Wagons were valuable property.

Distant neighing sent Slocum into a gunfighter's crouch. His Colt slipped into his hand, and he waited to see who approached.

More evidence that road agents hunting for something special had robbed this shipment was trotting toward him. The freighter had used a team of four horses. Three were returning to see if the furor was over so they could get back to pulling the freight wagon.

Serious road agents would never have allowed the team to get away. The horses were more valuable than anything likely to be carried in the cargo.

Unless you were a chemist and needed to brew up more explosive.

Slocum found the outlaws' trail, and began walking along, making certain at every turn that he did not lose them. They tried their usual tricks, going into a stream and staying on rocky patches, but Slocum saw a notch in the hills ahead and knew they were heading for that. Once they were past the break in the mountains, the terrain grew rockier and afforded any number of hiding places for a man not wanting to be found.

By mid-afternoon, Slocum was positive the small band was headed for the notch, and rode directly for it. He crossed into grassland that soon turned into a strong upslope and mountains. The outlaws' trail disappeared on him, but Slocum sniffed the air and caught a nose-wrinkling whiff of the witch's brew that Greeley concocted floating on an early evening breeze. He homed in on this, and soon found a worn trail leading to a small cabin.

Dark smoke curled from the stovepipe and was caught by the wind. Slocum retreated a quarter mile, found his horse a grassy patch to graze, then returned to the cabin on foot. He approached from higher on the mountainside so he could look down on it. He was immediately glad that he did. Two outlaws had been posted some distance from the cabin. If he had tried to sneak closer to the cabin, they would have not only spotted him, but also caught him in a deadly cross fire. If Warren Lester had chosen this spot as a hideout, he was smarter than Slocum thought.

Settling down with a large rock to his back, Slocum watched as Greeley's assistant entered and left the cabin with some regularity. The best Slocum could tell, the assistant went to a stockpile of chemicals out in the woods near the cabin and returned with a few bottles each time for his boss. At least, Slocum assumed Greeley was inside the cabin. At no time until it grew too dark to see clearly had anyone but the assistant entered or left, yet the amount of smoke billowing from the stovepipe grew in both volume and odor. A moon slowly rose over the trees, providing wan light.

Slocum wiped his nose on his sleeve when a breeze carried some of the smoke in his direction. His eyes burned, and he fought back a hard sneeze.

He wasn't sure how long he ought to maintain this vigil since he didn't see anything new. If Sarah Beth was anywhere around the cabin, she remained hidden from his sight. The outlaws had their horses corralled twenty yards into the woods, somewhere near the stockpile of chemicals the assistant raided every now and then. He could hear their feet stomping.

Just as Slocum got bored with watching and had decided to move to get a better look into the lit cabin, the door opened and Lawrence Greeley came out. The young man stretched, threw back his head, and howled like some wild animal. The sheer viciousness locked in that cry sent a cold shiver up Slocum's spine. Even worse, Greeley laughed like a madman.

Lester came out of the cabin and said something to him. Slocum was too far away to catch the words, but they argued until Greeley cocked his fist to throw a punch at the outlaw. Lester pushed the chemist away with one hand and drew his six-shooter with the other, intending to shoot.

Slocum hunkered down when Sarah Beth came from the cabin and pleaded with her brother. Again, the words were indistinct, but she was distraught and speaking only to Greeley, although Lester had his six-gun drawn and aimed at the man's head.

"Go to hell," came clearly to Slocum. Greeley shoved Lester, although the outlaw still held a gun on him. Then Greeley laughed again, a hideous, demented laugh that hardly sounded human.

Greeley spun abruptly and walked to the edge of the clearing some fifteen feet from the cabin.

"Yarrow, bring it out!"

Greeley's assistant came from the cabin, walking slowly,

holding something in his hand. Slocum strained to get a better look, but couldn't. Whatever the assistant carried caused his hands to shake uncontrollably. Greeley rebuked the man for such cowardice. Slocum caught a few words here and there. Yarrow almost ran back to the cabin when Greeley took whatever he carried.

"A demonstration. Witness," Greeley said as if he spoke to an arena filled with admirers. For a chilling moment, Slocum thought Greeley had discovered him. The chemist looked directly at him, holding out his hand as if offering a gift.

"Be careful, Lawrence," cautioned Sarah Beth. "This is very dangerous."

"Using true power is always dangerous, my dear," he said. "Controlling such awesome power is what I do."

Greeley placed what couldn't have been more than a match-head-sized object on the stump. He drew a knife with a long, slender blade and began gouging out the wood, sending chips flying. When he was satisfied, he dropped the match head into the hole.

"You sure this is gonna work, Kid?" Lester looked over Greeley's shoulder, as if afraid to go closer. Slocum found it curious that Greeley did not object to being called "kid." From what Sarah Beth had said, Greeley had been the youngest, weakest, and probably most picked on all his life. If anything, he puffed up at being called this.

"Watch and learn from a true genius," Greeley said.

He snatched Lester's pistol from the outlaw's hand, opened the gate, and knocked out a cartridge. He stuffed this into the hole he had cut in the stump, plugging up whatever he had dropped in. Nonchalantly, Greeley handed the six-shooter back to Lester and said, "Can you hit the ass end of that bullet?"

"I'm a good enough shot to shoot out a gnat's eye at a hundred paces," Lester said. "What'll happen?" His bravado faded as he stared at the stump.

"Do it," Greeley said. "Shoot out the gnat's *left* eye."

Lester snorted in contempt, cocked his six-gun, and fired. The foot-long tongue of orange flame leaped toward the stump. Then the stump exploded with a fury Slocum had seldom seen. Splinters flew outward like daggers. One even nicked his cheek, and he was more than fifty feet away, high up in the rocks. Slocum touched his injured cheek. His fingers came away sticky with his own blood.

He paid the pain no heed. He couldn't make out the details with a cloud of dust all around, but he did see that the stump had simply disappeared. Along with it had gone a three-foot radius of earth. In its place was a deep crater that a dozen sticks of dynamite couldn't have excavated. Greeley had wrought all this carnage with something no larger than the tip of Slocum's little finger.

"It's the most powerful explosive ever invented," Greeley boasted. "Hell, for all I know it's the most powerful explosive that *can* be invented."

"You sure it'll work? When we need it to?"

"You saw my demonstration. I used only a pinch. Imagine a lump of explosive the size of my fist." Greeley laughed nastily. "That's about the size of your brain."

Slocum saw Lester tense and his gun hand move to lift his six-shooter, but the outlaw holstered it instead. Whatever they planned, Lester needed Greeley's expertise—and a huge lump of the explosive.

Slocum had seen enough. It was time for him to move closer so he could get Sarah Beth out after the others went to sleep. From here, they could ride to Salt Lake City. She could alert the federal marshal there of whatever Lester planned, make a deal for her brother's testimony, and be free of the outlaws.

That was what he planned. What didn't fit into any of his schemes was the distinctive metallic click of a six-shooter cocking not five feet behind him. Slocum looked over his shoulder and saw a third outlaw with his gun trained on his back.

15

"Who the hell are you?"

Slocum turned slightly and kept his side toward the outlaw to give as small a target as possible. Since he hadn't been gunned down out of hand, he had a small chance of talking his way out of being captured.

"I was looking for Greeley," he said. "I got all turned around from directions he gave me."

"Greeley? You mean the Kid?"

"Lawrence Greeley," Slocum said, nodding. "The Kid."

"Ain't nobody supposed to know 'bout this place," the outlaw said. He scowled as he thought on the matter some, and this gave Slocum all the opening he was likely to get—or need. With a quick motion, he scooped up a handful of pebbles and tossed them at the outlaw. The man yelped, and then was silenced as Slocum pushed him to the ground and shoved his forearm down hard across the man's throat. After the gurgling stopped, Slocum let up on the pressure. He had crushed the man's windpipe.

Slocum got to his feet and looked back down into the camp at where the stump had been blasted apart and shook his head.

"The Kid?" Slocum laughed harshly. He didn't know what was going on, but if he wanted to get out of here with a whole skin, he had to act while he held the advantage of surprise. It wouldn't be too long before Lester discovered one of his sentries was missing. Slocum glanced back at the man sprawled gracelessly on the ground to make sure he wasn't going anywhere. The lack of any rise and fall of his chest convinced Slocum he had done his work well.

Moving downhill, Slocum got behind the cabin, but had no way of looking inside. He drew his knife and began whittling away at the mud between the logs, but stopped when he heard someone approaching from the direction of the wooded area to the north of the cabin. If he stayed, he would be seen in spite of deepening shadows. He lit out, going south into a ravine to hide before doing some more scouting of the area.

Two outlaws came up, arguing over tending the horses. Both went into the cabin.

An idea came to Slocum. He followed the high-banked ravine a ways, slithered out like a snake, and then circled to get to the woods where Lester's men had apparently stashed their horses. As he approached, the horses neighed loudly and pawed at the air. He went to cut their reins and send them racing off into the woods, but a gruff voice stopped him.

"What's with you mangy critters?"

Rising from where he had been sleeping came another outlaw. Slocum faded back into the woods and waited for the man to go back to sleep. Instead, the burly outlaw went to the horses and calmed them one by one, and then hitched up his gun belt and prowled around, more alert than Slocum liked.

Nothing was working for Slocum, so he headed back to the cabin. Without a good idea of how many men he faced in Lester's gang, he was going to keep getting into trouble. Eventually, it would do him in, and then Sarah Beth would be under her brother's thumb for good. If he got her away for even a short time, he knew he could talk some sense into her. She had to see that Greeley and Lester were plotting something more dangerous than even killing three men in a stagecoach before blowing the strongbox to hell and gone.

A game path ran back toward the cabin. Slocum hadn't gone a dozen paces when he felt something break against the top of his boot. He looked down and saw a thread whipping about like a snake. The explosion that followed lifted him like a rag doll and smashed him into a tree so hard, it knocked the wind out of him. The world went black all around him.

Slocum was aware of pain before he was of returning light. Every breath drove a knife into his chest. When he tried to move, he found he wasn't strong enough. As his eyes opened and focused, he saw this wasn't the problem. He was plenty strong, but the ropes around his ankles and wrists were stronger.

"You turn up in the damnedest places, Slocum," Lawrence Greeley said. His boyish face hovered a few inches away. Slocum surged and tried to break the ropes so he could smash his fist into Greeley's smirk.

"Now, now, don't hurt yourself," Greeley taunted.

"You booby-trapped the game trail," Slocum rasped out. Every word was pure agony, but the pain slowly receded in his chest as air rushed back into his lungs.

"Of course I did. I used only this much of my explosive." Greeley snapped his fingers and then indicated the tip of his little finger. "More than that would have blasted a crater ten feet deep. I didn't want that. All I wanted was to catch snoops. Or maybe a deer. The explosive would have blown it apart, true, but what remained would have made for good eating."

"Shut up, Kid," came a cold command from behind Slocum. Twisting about let him see Warren Lester, checking the cartridges in his six-shooter. "Can I kill him now?"

"You taking orders from a boy now, Lester?" Slocum wanted to play for time. Getting the two men fighting was his only hope of living even a few more minutes.

"The Dynamite Kid isn't a boy," Lester said. "He's got

smarts. He's made the most powerful dynamite in the world."

"I've told you, Lester, I've told you over and over. This is *not* dynamite. It is something more."

Slocum swallowed hard when he saw the size of the grayish lump Greeley held aloft like an Indian with a newly taken scalp. If a tiny dot of the explosive had blown the stump into splinters, a gob this size could level a mountain.

"You see?" Greeley walked around juggling the explosive. "Slocum understands how powerful this is, even if you fail to realize its potential."

"I know what it can do," Lester said, irritated by Greeley's attitude. "You've shown me enough times. Like when you cremated everything in the strongbox."

"I used a touch too much, that's all," Greeley said. "I wanted to use a speck, but you insisted on seeing it at its most dangerous."

"So it's my fault?"

Slocum said nothing. Let the two men fight. His only chance of getting away was if Lester killed Greeley and then left. Even as the thought crossed his mind, Slocum knew that wasn't going to happen. If Lester shot down the chemist, he would use his next round on Slocum.

And if Greeley killed Lester, Slocum was definitely a goner.

"Help me with my little demonstration," Greeley said, his mercurial mood shifting again. For him, it was as if the argument hadn't begun. "I need you to be certain Slocum is securely tied in place so he can see the window."

The single cabin window was on the west side. A ray of sun sneaked through and warmed the floor. Greeley pulled a crate over and made a show of positioning it so it was just out of the ray of sunlight. He slapped the blob of explosive onto the box and smeared it around.

"My invention is quite versatile, Slocum," Greeley said. "It can be detonated in several ways. You have seen the way electricity sets it off. It's very efficient."

"I saw Lester detonate a piece of it to blow the stump apart," Slocum said.

"Ah, you've spied on us for a while." Greeley shot Lester a cold look. "Your guards fell down on the job. I want you to take care of that." Greeley paused, glanced at Slocum, considered what he saw, and then laughed harshly. "Never mind, Warren. I think Slocum has already disciplined your malfeasant guard."

"I'll make sure it doesn't happen again."

"What are you getting out of this, Lester?" Slocum saw how the outlaw forced himself to remain civil to a wet-behind-the-ears kid. Call him the Dynamite Kid all he wanted, but Lester thought of his partner as a nuisance.

"Shut up," the outlaw said.

"You're so right, Warren," Greeley went on. "There's no need to let him know everything. But I will tell you this, Slocum. I've used this cabin to concoct a new batch of my explosive. Several pounds of it."

"So you killed the pharmacist in Sage Junction to keep him from telling anyone?"

"He was a fool. He refused to sell me what I wanted."

"So you killed him and stole it?"

"Something like that, but he didn't have enough on his shelves."

"So you stole a shipment of the chemicals coming from Salt Lake City."

"My, you have been busy, haven't you?"

"That's how he found us," said Lester. "He followed us from where we killed the freighter. I told you we shoulda hid our trail better, maybe heading in a different direction 'fore circling back. It's a good thing you agreed to come here first instead of to your laboratory. Don't fool around this time, Kid. Snuff out his wick good and proper."

"I think you are right, Warren." Greeley pursed his lips. "I had some regrets about killing him before. Not now."

"You haven't made more of your explosive," Slocum said, looking around the cabin. "Not yet and not here. There isn't any equipment. I don't know what you need, but you haven't set up to make any more."

"He's too damned smart," Lester growled. He lifted his six-gun to plug Slocum.

"Don't do that. I'll take care of him in my own fashion." Greeley pressed the grayish explosive all over the top of the crate. "You see what's in this wood box, Slocum? It is some useless dynamite. I say it is useless since my explosive is so much better, but I am not one to see it go to waste."

"I say we keep it. We might need it," Lester said.

"No!" Greeley pulled himself up to his full height, but still looked like a petulant child. "We won't need it. I'll have all we need after I get my laboratory set up."

"Why didn't you do it here?" Slocum asked.

"Because of snoops like you," Lester said. "We got a nice hideout. The Kid's making the explosive there, aren't you, Greeley?"

"I will not waste the case of dynamite Lester's men took from the cargo. They weren't able to grasp the concept of anything being more powerful." Greeley spun and took a magnifying glass from his vest pocket. He used a thin roll of his explosive to fasten it to the window.

"What're you doing?" Lester grew increasingly nervous watching his partner play with the explosive.

"As I was telling Slocum, my explosive detonates from electricity or impact. Heat also sets it off. When the sun dips low enough, say, an hour before sundown, it will let in a focused beam of light that will detonate my explosive on the crate of dynamite." Greeley silently put his hands together and then mimicked an explosion.

"Let me put a bullet in him now."

"He'll be dead in an hour or so. I want him to repent for his sins. Get the horses, Warren."

The outlaw grumbled, but left. Greeley came over until his face was only an inch from Slocum's.

"I want you to suffer. I want you to think about what you did to my sister and know that I can take care of her."

"She's tired of being your nursemaid," Slocum said. "She's finally decided she wants a man."

"If that man is you, Mr. Slocum, then she will have ever so much of you to dote on because you'll be blown into a million pieces!"

Slocum started to tell Greeley to go to hell, but he was too late. The self-styled Dynamite Kid had turned to go, trailing Warren Lester. He paused in the doorway, smiled viciously, and mockingly touched the brim of his hat as he left. The door slammed behind him, leaving Slocum alone in the cabin with the sun slowly sinking in the sky to touch the edge of the magnifying glass.

Working hard, he tried to scoot across the floor and kick the dynamite crate out of the path of the burning-hot beam. He got only a couple inches, finding that he was secured to a post driven into the floor. Slocum struggled to pull the post loose, but it was buried too deep for that. Frantic, he looked at the window. The top edge of the magnifying glass lit up now with the rays of the sun.

He kicked hard, and cried in pain as the ropes cut into his wrists. Straining, he stretched out as far as he could, thrusting his feet toward the crate. He missed by inches, but hope flared. If he could get his feet into the path of the burning beam, he might sear off the rope before it reached the explosive on the dynamite.

His heart sank when he realized the sun ray was working against him, starting close to the wall and moving out into the room toward the crate. He was staked out in the wrong place to ever get the rope into the searing light.

The beam inched closer. Slocum caught his breath as he waited to die. Then the concentrated sun's ray disappeared. A cloud had crossed the sun.

Slocum scooted back and gripped the post clumsily with both hands. He heaved and rocked and strained until he thought his tendons would rupture from the effort. When the post came free from the ground, he tumbled over. He kept rolling and smashed hard into the door. It was latched. Still holding the post in his hands, he wiggled around and began driving the sharpened tip into the ropes binding his ankles. He worked frantically when he saw the beam brightening. The cloud was moving on to reveal the hot afternoon sun once more.

Slocum cried out in relief when the rope gave way. His hands were still bound behind him, but his feet were free. He rolled over, got to his feet, and turned to lift the latch. He felt the blood rush from his brain, turning him faint, when he saw the edge of the dynamite crate begin to sizzle and pop as the light passing through the magnifying glass set it ablaze.

His numbed fingers found the latch. He spun and fell outside onto his knees. He regained his balance, got to his feet, and ran as hard as he could for the edge of the woods, vaulting over the crater where the stump used to be. Panting harshly, he reached the safety of the woods. A laugh escaped his lips. A heavy cloud hid the sun. If he was any judge, that lead-bottomed cloud promised rain later in the evening.

Rubbing his bonds against the rough bark of a piñon eventually freed him. He sank down, his back to the cabin with the tree trunk protecting him. He felt too shaky at his brush with death to immediately leave to fetch his horse. Strength slowly returned.

Then it felt as if he had stepped off a precipice and plunged downward.

"Lawrence? Are you in there, Lawrence?"

Slocum twisted about, and saw Sarah Beth going to the cabin door. Her hand rested on the latch, but she hesitated.

"There's dynamite inside!" Slocum shouted. "It'll go off. Run!"

"What? John? Where'd you come from?"

She didn't move and didn't understand what he said and she would die unless—

Slocum dug in the toes of his boots and ran back to the cabin, taking in a million small details all in a rush. The set of the woman's body told him she wasn't going to budge.

The clouds parted and let through a glimmer of sunlight. The scent of smoldering wood inside reached his nostrils. The cabin again became a deadly trap.

"Run. It's going to blow up. The cabin's a bomb!"

He reached for her. His strong arm circled her waist and swept her off her feet. Staggering, they headed back toward the woods.

The clouds parted and brilliant afternoon sunlight poured down on them.

The explosion lifted Slocum and Sarah Beth into the air and threw them forward with contemptuous ease.

16

Slocum smelled something burning. He shook his head, but nothing rattled around inside. He tried to lift his arms, but something pinned them to the ground. Then the ground wiggled sinuously under him and a distant voice said, "Get off me!"

He blinked hard and forced his eyes open. His face was only an inch away from Sarah Beth's.

"You're on fire!"

She'd shouted, and the words slowly fit together with what he knew from his other senses. Pain on his back, the odor of burned flesh, the explosion! It all came together in a rush. He pulled his hands in and pressed Sarah Beth hard to his body as he rolled onto his back. Pain seared his senses, and he knew his shirt had been set on fire by the blast. He rolled again and again, holding Sarah Beth close, just to be sure. When the explosion had plucked them off their feet, he had grabbed and held her before landing on top of her. His back had protected the woman but had paid the price.

He stopped rolling, and then lay on his back with her body weighing him down. The last of the smoldering specks on his vest were finally snuffed out.

Sarah Beth's lips moved, but Slocum couldn't hear her.

"What? What'd you say?"

"We're both deaf from the loud bang," she shouted. Part of the words got through to him, but he realized he had read her lips for the complete message.

Slocum pushed her to one side and sat up. The cabin had simply disappeared. When Greeley's explosion had detonated the dynamite, it had been cataclysmic. Wood had simply vanished, and what hadn't vanished had been driven outward in flights of flaming arrows. He realized now that some of those splinters were embedded in his back. He tried not to groan, but he did.

"You're hurt," Sarah Beth said. Before he could protest, she spun him around. He heard her gasp. Then there was only a loud ringing in his ears.

She got to her feet, and he stood up unsteadily, letting her help him. He had successfully protected her from the worst of the blast and she had come through almost unscathed, but he had borne the brunt of the explosion. Sarah Beth took him by the hand and tugged. For a moment, he resisted, then allowed her to lead him from the destruction that had almost stolen away both their lives.

At first, he thought she was dazed and wandering aimlessly. Then he realized she was taking him toward a creek running near the cabin.

"I can hear," she shouted in his ear. He only nodded. If he tried to answer, he would shout. "Take off your shirt. No, wait, let me do it."

He started to protest, then let her gingerly strip off his coat, vest, and shirt for him. The splinters had nailed his clothing to his body. Sarah Beth gently plucked one wood spike after another from his back. Just when the pain got to the point where he wished he had a bottle of whiskey to kill the sensation, she finished.

"Into the water. It'll wash off the blood and grime."

Slocum knew it would chill his flesh, too, and numb it enough so he wouldn't cry out if she touched him. He hesitated, then decided she wasn't going to see anything she hadn't already seen. Stripping off what remained of his clothes, he stepped completely naked into the stream. Near the bank, it went up to his calves. Farther out, it sloshed around his waist. Slocum leaned back and floated on the rapidly running stream. He almost passed out as the water touched his injured back, but Sarah Beth again came to his rescue. Her arm slid under his head and supported him so he wouldn't drown.

He regained his senses and turned toward her. The water had plastered her blouse to her bosom in a delightful fashion. Watching her breasts bob gently on the surface of the water enticed him more and more. He turned his head and pursed his lips as one breast came closer. He found the hard little nubbin on the tip and sucked it into his mouth, and was rewarded with a tiny gasp of pleasure.

"Oh, John, you're so forward." Even as she sounded so modest, her hand stroked over his belly and lower until she found something to play with. Her fingers circled his growing hardness and teased him to full erection.

With her hand delightfully stroking up and down, he turned his attention to her other breast and the hard nipple popped up there. His tongue shoved out fast, driving the penny-sized button of flesh down into the softness below. Sarah Beth groaned even more now. Slocum floated around, letting her still support his head with one hand while her other hand moved with increasing urgency on him. He reached underwater and found her leg. His hand slipped beneath her clinging skirt and upward, stroking over her fleshy thigh until he found the spot that made her do more than groan.

She sobbed with need as his middle finger entered her and stirred about like a spoon in a mixing bowl. Sarah Beth sagged down as desire possessed her. This caused Slocum's head to dip underwater and momentarily upend him. He sputtered and thrashed about until his feet pressed downward into the slippery river bottom. He kept his finger firmly within her heated center while reaching around her waist with his other hand to cup a firm buttock.

They stood together in the water, her hand tugging insistently to move him toward the spot where his finger resided so warmly.

"What do you want?" he asked. He nibbled at her ear as he whispered.

"You know. Don't tease me. I want you so!"

"Like this?" Slocum used the hand resting on her rump to pull up her skirt and expose her privates. She tugged him toward her, and they spent a few seconds thrashing about in the water to get into the proper position. Then Slocum straightened his knees and rocketed straight upward into seething carnal delight.

One instant, the rushing water around him kept his organ cool; the next, the sheath of female flesh caused his blood to boil. He put his arms around her waist and began moving her so she bobbed up and down on the water, sliding on and off him. Sarah Beth let out tiny sounds that grew from deep in her throat and finally sneaked free of her lips.

"So good," she gasped out.

"Let yourself go. Enjoy this. Scream, if you want."

"I . . . I shouldn't. It's not ladylike."

"It's not ladylike having a man do this to you either." He gripped both her ass cheeks and began lifting and pulling and twisting her all around. He tried to remain within her as he got her moving faster. Their crotches ground together underwater even as the river rushed past and stimulated them both.

Slocum forgot about the splinters still in his back. His loins burned with need. He stroked harder and deeper, and was met with her eager physical responses. Sarah Beth gave as good as she got—and they both won.

Throwing himself backward as he lifted caused the dark-haired woman to cry out in surprise. She was astraddle him as he floated on his back in the river. Slocum held on tight and moved up and down as hard as he could. He felt the warmth turning to fire, and then he erupted. They clung together and rolled over and over in the water. Sarah Beth's legs locked around his waist until there was no more need.

Weakly, she released him and drifted on the current. Slocum stroked toward her and tweaked a nipple sticking up out of the water.

"That feels so good," she said. "I'm still tingling all over."

"So . . . ladylike," he said.

She looked hard at him, as if he might be mocking her. She saw he wasn't, and laughed.

"You continue to surprise me, John. You're not like anyone else I've ever met."

"Chances are good you haven't met too many men, other than your brother," he said.

She turned away and idly paddled to a spot a few feet away. He couldn't tell if a tear had formed because of the river washing across her face.

"You might be right," she said. "But Lawrence needs someone to look after him. He's bright, but he doesn't have a lot of common sense."

"He won't learn to get by on his own if you always clean up after him," Slocum said.

"I don't have anyone else," she said. "Our parents died in a horrible fire when he was only twelve. I've looked after him ever since."

"What's that? Ten years?"

"Nine," she said. "I hoped he would do well in school and be on his own, but he was expelled for reasons other than academic."

"He wouldn't take shit off anyone and always wanted his own way," Slocum said.

"That's crudely put," she said.

"But accurate."

She nodded numbly. She rolled onto her side and then dog-paddled to him. Once more, they wrapped arms around one another.

"He needs more help than I can give him now," she said. "Please, John, it won't be too much. I need you to help him."

"He tried to blow me up in the cabin. *You* would have gotten blown to Kingdom Come if I hadn't rescued you. He doesn't care who he kills."

"He's fallen in with bad company."

"From what I can see, he's leading them. Warren Lester's a cold-blooded killer, and yet he's willing to follow your brother's lead." Slocum snorted, and expelled some water from his nose. "The Dynamite Kid, Lester called him. Greeley enjoyed it."

"He encourages it," Sarah Beth said sadly. "It appeals to his romantic nature. He's still so much like a little boy reading the penny dreadfuls. He might be a genius, but he has his fantasies."

"They're going to get him killed," Slocum said. If someone else didn't get to Lawrence Greeley before him, Slocum would see that the Dynamite Kid came to a sudden and fatal end. He remembered the glee on Greeley's face, followed by the utter hatred, as he set up the magnifying glass to detonate the explosives. He wasn't a man led astray as much as a demented killer finding his inspiration from some cesspool deep inside his own soul.

"He doesn't have to die," she said.

"He killed the owner of the Crazy Eights Saloon in Sage Junction," Slocum said suddenly. He wanted to gauge Sarah Beth's reaction. He wasn't disappointed. She looked even glummer as she nodded agreement. "Why'd he kill Allen?"

"He didn't mean to do that. He wanted to get even for the way that awful man humiliated him. But it happened."

"That's why you busted me out of jail. You knew I had nothing to do with either the fire or killing Allen."

Again, she nodded. She would have shed tears, but the river water broke against her cheek and carried away any such display of sorrow.

Slocum began kicking lightly, steering them for the bank. He was getting cold from the water sucking at his body warmth. When he got his feet under him and walked out, he saw the goose flesh through Sarah Beth's soaked clothing. She shivered so hard, her teeth began to chatter.

"Get out of those clothes," he said. She looked sharply at him. "I'll build a fire and dry them. Otherwise, you'll catch your death of a cold." Slocum saw from her reaction that whatever had been between them, no matter how brief and intimate, was now gone. Whether she'd made love to him to secure his help with her brother, or whether she'd felt anything more for him, wasn't a question he could answer.

It wasn't a question he wanted to answer.

Naked, he padded around and gathered wood. When the fire blazed warmly, he washed his filthy clothes and laid them out to dry next to Sarah Beth's. Under other circumstances, sitting naked next to an equally naked beauty would have to be the closest thing to heaven he was likely to find on earth. But not now. She sat with her arms wrapped around herself, hunched forward, her hair dangling down in damp strings to curtain her face.

Slocum silently shook out his clothes and began dressing. His mind raced. He wasn't going to let Greeley get away with trying to kill him the way he had, but killing the self-styled Dynamite Kid would never get him off the hook with Marshal Pritchard in Sage Junction. Slocum needed Greeley to confess to the arson and murder—and he couldn't do that dead.

"Where is he?" Slocum said, sitting back down on the log opposite Sarah Beth. The fire between them caused a heat shimmer that made her appear to be unreal, a vision, a naked, lovely vision.

She looked up. Her blue eyes were bloodshot from crying.

"I heard him talking with Lester about a bank robbery. I'm not sure where."

Slocum considered the nearby towns, and decided none of them fit the bill for a man out to make a reputation for himself.

"The biggest gold supply's up at the Shady Lady Mine."

He saw Sarah Beth stiffen and then draw into herself even more.

"What do you know about that?" Slocum asked.

"He stole the gold. Lawrence took the gold."

"When the wall got blown off, there wasn't anything inside."

"He'd already taken it, but he didn't get any thrill out of it. It was too easy, he said. He used tiny specks of his explosive to blow out nails. Turned them to vapor, he said, making it easy to lift the boards away. He only needed to do that to a couple panels and then remove the gold."

"He wasn't very clever about it," Slocum said.

"He didn't *have* to blow up the entire building!"

"I meant, there was another wagonload of gold coming up from the smelter. If he'd waited a day, he could have stolen twice as much."

"He still got a hundred pounds," she said.

"And that wasn't good enough," Slocum said in disgust. If *he* had robbed Snell's warehouse of that much gold, his only concern would have been getting it the hell out of Wyoming and going somewhere where he could spend it. Being too easy to steal or not making a big enough bang when the vault was breached would have had nothing to do with the satisfaction of being rich.

"He doesn't need the money," Sarah Beth said. "We're not rich, but he makes some money off other inventions."

"The Dynamite Kid just wants to watch things blow up," Slocum said. He reached over and patted Sarah Beth's clothing to be sure it was dry, then handed over her blouse and skirt. She silently took them, then got all modest on him. He looked away as she dressed.

"He's done terrible things to you, I know, John. I've tried to make up for them."

"I'm wanted in Sage Junction for arson and murder, and the owner of the Shady Lady Mine thinks I stole his gold. Even if I found what your brother did with Snell's gold and tried to return it, I'd get strung up before I could explain."

"He'll only get worse," she said simply.

Slocum agreed with that. Left to his own devices, Lawrence Greeley would go on a rampage that would leave dozens of people dead or maimed in his wake. The worst of it was that Greeley would do it for the thrill of the destruction rather than to steal gold. There was a limit to how much gold a man could carry, but rabid, mad-dog viciousness only fed on itself.

Slocum sat and thought harder. The banks in Border and Sage Junction were jokes. Whatever they had in them could be robbed without expending more than a few fired bullets and a lot of loud yelling. Holding up a stagecoach wouldn't appeal to Greeley any longer either. He had already done that, and blasted apart the strongbox so that everything inside was charred. The killing might have excited him, but three men dying would have to be topped with even more deaths. Greeley had already taken the Shady Lady Mine gold. Then a glimmering of an idea came to Slocum.

Snell knew better than to leave his gold in the Sage Junction bank, and always freighted it to Salt Lake City. It had been a spell since Slocum had ridden through that Mormon town, but he remembered it as orderly and filled with banks. If Greeley wanted to make a name for himself as the Dynamite Kid, he couldn't go far wrong riding into Salt Lake City and blowing up a couple of the bigger banks.

With Warren Lester and his gang to back him, getting the loot from the banks wouldn't be difficult. There was no need for subtlety. If anything, Greeley wanted the notoriety, and would set off his blasts when there were the most witnesses around. The more people to watch, the more likely he was to kill dozens.

Slocum turned grim thinking of how pleased this would make Lawrence Greeley.

"I'm going to Salt Lake City," Slocum said. Sarah Beth looked up. He couldn't read the expression on her pale face. He might as well have told her he liked green apples or skipping stones across a lake.

He left her beside the fire as he went to find his horse and get on the trail of the Dynamite Kid.

17

Slocum used a twig to draw a crude map in the dirt to orient himself. The Shady Lady Mine and Border were to his north and Sage Junction to the south, with the main road heading west toward Salt Lake City. He tried to figure from the lay of the land where Greeley's hideout was. It wasn't likely to be far from the cabin that had blown up and almost taken him and Sarah Beth through the Pearly Gates.

After a few minutes of intense study, he tossed the stick to the ground in disgust and then erased the dirt map with his boot. Without a decent trail to follow, he had no way of finding Greeley or Lester. The lure of a bank to rob would be enough to keep Lester and his gang trailing after Greeley like puppy dogs, but eventually, Greeley had to deliver. No bank worth even a stick of dynamite lay within a few days' ride, so Greeley had to be going to Salt Lake City.

As Slocum had figured.

His thoughts turned to the lovely woman, and he wondered what would happen to Sarah Beth after he had it out with her brother. Leaving her had been easy enough, but Slocum had second thoughts on the matter now. Her entire life was wrapped up in Lawrence, touting his so-called genius to anyone who would listen and fixing the problems he caused. Slocum wished he had proof of his own innocence in Allen's death and the Crazy Eights fire, but more than this, he wanted Snell over at the mine to think well of him and not consider him a murderer and thief. The mine owner had helped him when he needed it and was a decent fellow.

Slocum mounted and started the long ride to Salt Lake City, leaving behind a passel of people thinking ill of him. It wasn't the first time he had turned his back on such woe, and it wouldn't be the last time he rode away either. Without realizing he did it, Slocum rubbed his neck where the rough hemp rope had been looped. Sarah Beth had saved him from hanging, and she had saved him from rotting in the Sage Junction jail until the circuit judge had come by to sentence him to hang. Rescuing her from the exploding cabin had evened one score, but he wondered how far he had to go to even the other.

All day, the sun beat down on him, at first on his back and then on his face, keeping his pace slow and his thirst great. More often than he liked, he let his horse have its head to find a trickle of water. The longer he traveled, the harder it was finding water. Salt Lake City was smack dab in the middle of a desert with a lake so salty it would gag anyone drinking it. If it hadn't been for the hard work and extensive irrigation bringing water down into the town from higher in the Wasatch Mountains, the city would never have prospered.

By the time he reached the gleaming jewel in the desert, he still had not decided what he owed Sarah Beth. She wanted him to rescue her brother, but Slocum was more inclined to shoot the son of a bitch on sight. A dog might be loving and good to have around, but if it turned rabid, the only cure was a bullet in the head. Lawrence Greeley had turned more than rabid. A dog foaming at the mouth was crazy and out of control, not knowing what it did and mindlessly striking out at anyone or anything around it. Greeley, in his persona as the Dynamite Kid, was calculating in his viciousness. He had tasted blood and liked it. That made him worse than rabid.

Brilliant and wanting to kill made for a bad combination.

The broad streets beckoned, and Slocum rode down the center of one, appreciating the spacious town. Most frontier towns huddled together, one building holding up the next, with buildings often sharing walls to save on construction material and costs. Salt Lake City was richer than that, with eye-appealing architecture, dominated by the tabernacle in the center of town, which oversaw all commerce. A huge golden angel wobbled slightly in the wind atop the main spire, and reflected eye-searing rays from the desert sun.

"Where do I look for them?" Slocum asked, knowing the angel was not going to respond.

Slocum sat bolt upright in the saddle when he heard a distant explosion and saw a column of dark smoke rising not a quarter mile away. He put his heels to his horse's flanks, breaking into a trot, wondering if the angel had answered his heartfelt question.

He slowed, and then sat and stared when he saw the volunteer firemen rushing to put out a blaze that threatened an entire block of stores.

"What happened?" he called to a man with soot smudging his face and looking more worried by the minute as the flames ate through the center store.

"My place, my pharmacy," the man moaned. "It blew up, just like the other places."

"What other places?"

The pharmacist waved his hands around, then rubbed his eyes, smearing the soot even more.

"For the past couple days, stores have been blowing up all over town. The chief of police thinks someone is setting fires, but I was coming back to my pharmacy when I saw it go *whoosh*!" He made a gesture like a fountain spewing into the sky. "It wasn't somebody careless with a cigar, that's for certain. This *blew* up."

"How do you mean? Like it had been dynamited?"

"That's it. A bomb went off, and I lost everything."

"What other places?" Slocum asked, but the pharmacist wandered off in a daze, muttering to himself and then when his shock abated, shouting at the firemen to work harder.

If Slocum had any doubt that Lawrence Greeley had headed for Salt Lake City, this erased it once and for all. The chemist must have stolen more supplies to make additional explosives, and then blown up the store to cover his theft. Slocum doubted anyone in Salt Lake City could make heads or tails of the chemicals stolen even if they did an inventory, much less guess how Greeley would put the chemicals together, but the man might have wanted to kill someone just for the fun of it. Covering a theft was less interesting to the Dynamite Kid than fire and murder.

"Anyone in the store?" Slocum yelled. Two women turned toward him, their parasols spinning nervously.

"My husband was inside," one woman said. Tears ran down her cheeks. "I had just stepped outside when the explosion destroyed everything."

"You see anybody around the pharmacy beforehand?"

"Are you a lawman? Do you know who did this?"

"I think it was an outlaw going by the name of Warren Lester," Slocum said. "Him and a youngster calling himself the Dynamite Kid did this same crime over in Sage Junction. Blew up a saloon, killed the owner, then did it all over again with the town apothecary." Slocum wanted to plant the seed that Greeley was responsible for Allen's death and the resulting saloon fire. If Marshal Pritchard ever moved his arthritic bones in this direction, he would find people convinced they knew who the real owlhoot was—and it wouldn't be John Slocum.

The other woman spoke up. "I saw a young man, with wild eyes and wearing fancy hand-tooled boots. He was out in the street when poor Mr. Young was blown up inside." She put a hand on her companion's arm. This started the one Slocum took to be Mrs. Young crying in earnest now.

Slocum rode closer until a uniformed policeman blew a whistle and held up a hand to stop him.

"No closer, mister. It's too dangerous."

"I was talking to Mrs. Young," Slocum said, jerking his thumb over his shoulder in the direction of the two women, "and she said this wasn't the first business to get blown up."

"Been a couple others. Mighty strange goings-on, if you ask me."

"Why not talk some with the widow and see if she has any ideas what might have happened?" Slocum knew it was better if the policeman heard Lester's name from a victim rather than some stranger who had just ridden into town.

"Reckon you're right," the policeman said. "Don't know what she could tell me, but there might be something."

"You might get a promotion if you nab whoever's responsible," Slocum said. This lent speed to the lawman's heels. The policeman almost ran to talk to Mrs. Young.

Slocum wished he had found out where the other stores Greeley had blasted were, but he knew that probably mattered less now than where the banks were in Salt Lake City. Lester wasn't going to let Greeley continue blowing up small businesses when all the money the gang could carry rested in a bank vault.

Slocum rode around a spell, then found the freight office with a familiar rig outside. He dismounted and found a cool spot to wait until Rourke and two others from the Shady Lady Mine left. They climbed into the wagon and got the mules pulling back in the direction of the distant mountains to the east. Slocum waited until he was sure they had been gone long enough not to return unexpectedly, then went to the depot office.

The clerk looked up over the tops of his half-glasses.

"What kin I do fer ya?"

Slocum saw two shotgun guards posted on either side of the room.

"I was hunting for Rourke, from Snell's mine."

"You jist missed the varmint. Said he was headin' back right away."

"I can understand that," Slocum said, "what with the trouble we've had at the Shady Lady recently."

"Can't say I was surprised that Windsor got his neck stretched," the clerk said. He glanced down at the ledger book in front of him. Slocum hoped the man didn't see how taken aback he was.

"I reckon Snell caught him with his hand in the till," said Slocum. "Don't matter the reason, if he got himself put six feet under."

"Something to do with a man named Rick gettin' hisself shot. Didn't hear the details, but Rourke's the top hand there now. That's why Snell sent him with the gold shipment rather than the usual driver."

The clerk closed the ledger. "Now, what kin I do fer ya?"

"I was supposed to tell Rourke to bring back some supplies," Slocum said, thinking fast. "Since I missed him here, might be I can catch him at the smithy. Snell wanted some chain and other hardware."

"Didn't say a word 'bout that," the clerk said.

"I'll track him down," Slocum said, starting to leave. As if he had a sudden thought, he stopped and said, "I heard tell of some buildings getting blown up. That so?"

"'Tis," the clerk said with a sigh. "A bunch of places have been destroyed in the past couple days. Heard that the police chief thinks it's one fella doing it all, though why he wants to just blow up buildings is a poser."

"Might be the work of the Dynamite Kid," Slocum said.

"Who's that?"

"A name I heard," Slocum said. "One last thing. Can you tell me what's the biggest bank in town?"

"Biggest? You mean the biggest building?"

"The one with the most money in it."

"Probably the same thing," the clerk said. Slocum noticed how edgy the two guards had become when he mentioned a bank. "Ride on down the street north 'bout a mile. The Deseret Bank."

"Much obliged." Slocum left quickly, not wanting to spend another second inside with the guards staring at him so hard they were boring holes in him. All it took was one of them to ask the police for a stack of wanted posters. But Slocum felt he had done well, planting Greeley's moniker where it would come up if the law started making inquiries.

More than this, though, he figured he had been cleared back at the Shady Lady Mine if they had hung Windsor for shooting down Rick. The foreman's entire web of deceit must have come undone. Slocum wasn't likely to return to find out if his name had been cleared since that was a needless risk. If he had been exonerated, though, that set well with him since Snell knew he had not befriended a thief and murderer.

Slocum rode in the direction the clerk had given, and found the bank easily. It had a white stone front, towered three stories above the street, and looked as imposing as any European castle. To storm this bank would require a small army of outlaws.

Or a big wad of Greeley's explosive.

Slocum rode around the building, trying to figure out where the explosive might be planted. He saw the imposing brick walls and guessed the vault inside was steel. Blasting through the brick would leave the vault unscathed unless Greeley intended to detonate two explosions. Or one colossal blast.

"What you doin'?"

Slocum looked around, trying to see who had spoken. His eyes slowly lifted to a balcony on the second floor where a uniformed guard with a rifle stood. The rifle wasn't aimed at Slocum—not exactly. It would take only a small shift to come into the alert guard's sights, though.

"Thought someone I knew was back here."

"Why'd anybody be in the alley behind the bank?"

Slocum started to say his mythical friend was sleeping off too much booze, then remembered this was a Mormon town and had only a few saloons tucked away at the outskirts. This close to the center of business, anyone stumbling along drunk would stick out like a clumsy carpenter's swollen thumb.

"I'm a federal marshal on the trail of an outlaw gang led by a man named Warren Lester. You ever hear of him?"

"Can't say I have. Lemme see your badge."

"What about the Dynamite Kid? You know of him? He's a young one with a flair for blowing up things."

"Do tell. Show me your badge." The guard's rifle swung around. He still didn't quite aim at Slocum, but was coming closer. From his vantage point on the walkway, he could command the entire alley behind the bank.

Before Slocum could think up a new lie that would satisfy the suspicious guard, his horse began crow-hopping. Slocum felt the deep, familiar rumble, and knew Greeley had detonated another batch of his explosive.

By the time the thunderous report sounded, Slocum was turned and ready to ride. The shock wave distracted the guard enough for Slocum to return to the main street without getting a bullet in his back. A crowd already rushed down the broad street in the direction of a fire. The curls of black smoke rising there told Slocum that Greeley had struck again.

"What was blown up?" Slocum kept shouting the question until a man answered.

"Looks to be the stage depot. Can't imagine what caused it."

Slocum galloped on and saw the blaze avidly devouring the depot. Two men lay stretched out in the street. From their lack of important limbs, there was no hope either had survived the explosion.

"He's around back tryin' to rob the stage," gasped out one man whose clothing told of nearness to the explosion. "I saw him. Shot down a driver and stole the strongbox."

This made no sense at all. Even a heavily laden stage-coach would hold a fraction of the gold the Deseret Bank had in its vault. Slocum hardly believed Greeley had come to his senses and scouted the bank, only to realize how difficult it would be to steal a dime from such a heavily guarded place. Without entering, Slocum knew the bank vault would be top of the line and impervious to most any illicit entry. For Greeley, that would be a challenge he could not refuse to meet.

The crowd grew. Some men started a bucket brigade to move water to the fire, but they had only a half dozen buckets and the flames leaped thirty feet or more into the air. It would be only a matter of minutes before the stage depot was completely gutted.

Slocum followed four policemen around to the rear. Again, he wondered what the hell was going on. He recognized one of Lester's men hammering away at the lock on a strongbox, making no attempt to escape. Even if the box held nothing but gold coins, it was too small to be worthwhile. Better to take the entire box and ride away to open it where the law wasn't swarming around.

"Get your hands up," ordered one policeman. He pulled back his blue jacket and drew the six-shooter holstered at his hip. The other policemen with him followed suit. Lester's henchman had four guns trained on him, but he didn't look worried.

"No need to get all pissy," the outlaw said. "You jist come a bit closer, why don't you, if you want to clap handcuffs on me?" He thrust out his wrists in invitation.

"You drop your gun first."

Slocum reached for his own six-shooter. Nothing about this was right.

"Drop your gun, or we'll cut you down where you stand."

"Do tell," the outlaw said. "You gonna want me to put this down, too?" He held out a pair of wires. The cut ends gleamed copper and bright in the afternoon sun.

"What's that? Put it down, too, or we'll shoot."

"Shoot now!" Slocum shouted. He lifted his six-gun to fire, but was too late. The outlaw touched the wires. On either side of him rose columns of dirt and rock that sent the policemen staggering away. The outlaw laughed, but not for long when Slocum opened fire. The first round missed, but Slocum connected with the second. The owlhoot grabbed his leg and dropped to one knee. He looked up, a puzzled expression on his face. He wasn't supposed to get shot.

"Grab some sky," Slocum shouted. The outlaw shook himself, as if this would clear his head.

"You let us do our job," a policeman said. The man's blue jacket was ripped and filthy from the blast.

"Don't get near him," Slocum warned. "He might have—"

This was as far as he got. The outlaw looked even more astounded at the turn of events as the ground shook. Slocum had felt this warning before and spun, hiding his face an instant before the shock hit him and knocked him to the ground. He scraped his knees and a few spots on his jacket smoldered, but he was alive.

That was more than could be said for three of the four policemen—and the outlaw.

18

Slocum swung around, six-shooter ready for action, but there was no one left to shoot. The outlaw had disappeared, and what remained of his body would have to be scraped up or mopped up to put into a pine box. The ringing in Slocum's ears turned into a loud, shrill tone.

It took him a few seconds to realize this wasn't caused by the explosion. He knelt beside the surviving policeman and said too loudly, "What's that sound?"

"Call whistle. Summoning more law, even volunteers."

"A posse?"

The policeman nodded, then winced at the pain. Slocum found himself being pushed aside as more police rushed to their fellow officer's aid. Stepping away, Slocum gathered his wits. The outlaw had not known the second detonation was going to kill him. The expression on his face an instant before he died told the story.

Poking around, Slocum found the severed wires the outlaw had run to a large lead-acid battery like those used in telegraph offices. Slocum laughed harshly. The outlaw had nothing to do with this. Lawrence Greeley had set this up, given the exposed leads to Lester's henchman, and told him what to do. The wires had blown up tiny specks of explosive buried on either side of the spot where the outlaw had tried so ineptly to open the strongbox. This diversion would keep police occupied for some time.

Slocum kept looking, and found another set of wires running off behind a distant building where someone— Greeley?—had set off the final blast killing the policemen and the outlaw. This had been planned if anything had gone wrong, and the dead outlaw knew nothing about it. Greeley didn't want the outlaw spilling his guts about what was really happening.

Checking the strongbox confirmed what Slocum had already guessed. The box contained some legal papers, a bundle of scrip that didn't amount to more than a hundred dollars, and nothing else. Such loot was beneath contempt for Warren Lester and his gang. For Greeley, it was worse than contemptible. It was downright insulting.

"You leave that money where it is, mister."

Slocum turned, and saw a uniformed guard with a rifle trained on him. He tried to remember where he had seen the man before.

"That there's property of the Deseret Bank, and I'm takin' it into custody."

"What are you doing here?" Slocum asked. "You're a guard at the bank."

"Heard the whistle. That's the signal fer ever' able-bodied man within hearin' to come runnin'. It's our civic duty. In this here case, it's business, too, since that money was destined to be put into the bank."

"How many other guards came when the police whistle sounded?"

The guard shrugged, then said, "Reckon all of us came runnin'. The blast, the call, it was what we've trained to do."

"Who's guarding the bank?"

The words hardly passed Slocum's lips when he felt the all-too-familiar temblor that preceded the airborne shock wave from Greeley's explosive. The bank guards who had come to the aid of the police stumbled about, dazed. Slocum didn't bother telling them they had been lured away from the real robbery. He vaulted into the saddle and galloped down the street, only to veer away from the bank when an explosion ripped a crater in the center of the street. Greeley had mined the approaches to the bank to keep police at bay, should any ignore the whistled message for help at the stagecoach depot.

Slocum stepped down from his horse and took the time to reload his six-shooter. He knew what he would face in the bank. Colt Navy pointed in front of him, Slocum squinted and plunged into the dust cloud that had settled around the bank. The front doors were barred on the inside. Slocum wiped off a spot on the glass and peered inside.

Four men sprawled on the floor. Slocum couldn't tell if they were dead, but they weren't moving around a whole lot. A new explosion inside shattered the glass in Slocum's face. Only luck kept him from being blinded by shards erupting outward. As it was, he staggered away and sat down hard in the street. Tiny scratches on his face bled profusely, but he ignored the pain and got to his feet. Entering the front way was out of the question, so Slocum went to the side of the bank.

He saw a nervous team of horses behind the bank, and knew a wagon was hitched up to carry the loot. Slocum advanced warily, and stopped before he reached the corner. The horses snorted and eyed him fearfully. The team almost bolted when another explosion shook the building.

"Get it all loaded, boys. We ain't got much time."

Slocum chanced a quick peek around the corner in time to see Lester pop through a hole in the rear of the building. The last blast had opened a hole large enough for the outlaw and two of his men to stumble through, carrying heavy boxes. It would have been easy enough to get the drop on them, but Slocum held back—and was glad he did. Above, on the balcony where the bank guard had stood earlier, another of the gang patrolled. The outlaw called down to

Lester, "They're comin' back, Boss. I see a dozen of 'em, all the deputies and more besides. You want me to take a shot at 'em?"

"No need," Greeley said, strutting out. He wore a linen duster pulled back to show a pair of six-guns slung at his hips. His fancy hand-tooled boots were covered with dirt, and a broad-brimmed black hat had turned almost white from dust. What held Slocum's attention was in the young man's hand. Greeley twisted the handle on the small dynamo. A low-pitched whir was almost instantly drowned out by a series of detonations in front of the bank.

"That ought to take care of them for a small time," Greeley said with some pleasure. "It's nice to be the Dynamite Kid."

"Glad you think so, Greeley," Lester said. He motioned for his men to continue loading the heavy crates into the rear of the wagon.

"Is it time?" Greeley asked.

"You take such pleasure in it," Lester said. "Go ahead."

Slocum aimed his pistol, then relaxed the finger on the trigger. Something was going on between the two outlaws that he didn't understand.

Greeley clumsily drew both his six-shooters and opened fire on the others in Lester's gang. His accuracy was less a factor in the men's deaths than the sheer amount of lead he threw in their direction. Three outlaws were taken by surprise, and never cleared leather to get their own weapons into play.

"You goddamn bushwhacker!" cried the lookout on the balcony. He swung his rifle around—and he died when Lawrence Greeley emptied both of his six-guns at him. The guard's fingers went limp, and then he tumbled to the ground with a thud. From the way he lay on the ground, there was no doubt he was dead.

"More for us," Lester said, grinning wolfishly.

"Let's get out of town before the lawmen figure out what has happened."

"You set the other bombs?"

"All over town," Greeley said. His grin was even more feral than the outlaw's. "Any time now, my timers will set off a dozen fires."

"You enjoy the notion of people getting blown up more than anything else, don't you?" Lester asked.

Slocum almost called out a warning to Greeley, but he held his tongue. He saw the way Lester's hand twitched just a little and how his fingers curled and opened.

"I enjoy killing far more than I ever thought," Greeley said. He was breathing heavily and his face was flushed with excitement. "They never understood me. I'm showing them all what genius can do."

"And I'll show you what a bullet in the gut can do," Lester said. His draw was smooth and his hand steady. "You're a sick son of a bitch. Killing you is going to be a civic duty."

Slocum almost called out again, this time to warn Lester. The look on Greeley's face was totally unexpected. He was enjoying this showdown even more than the prospect of blowing up half of Salt Lake City.

"Your own deeds deserve punishment, too, but being stupid, Lester, well, that's the ultimate crime."

"Go to hell, Dynamite Kid," Lester said sarcastically. He pulled the trigger and his pistol blew up in his hand.

Lester screeched and grabbed the stump remaining at the end of his arm.

Greeley chuckled as he took time to reload a six-gun. He closed the gate, spun the cylinder, and aimed at Lester.

"You left your sidearm untended earlier. That was stupid. I put a little of my marvelous explosive in the barrel, in case you tried to double-cross me."

"You stupid—" That was all Lester got out before Greeley shot him in the face.

"Drop your iron," Slocum said, seeing his opportunity and taking it. Greeley was still gloating over outwitting Lester and having the outlaw blow himself up.

"Slocum, I thought I had taken care of you. Did you paste yourself back together?"

"I saved your sister from falling into your trap," Slocum said. "You almost killed her."

"Poor Sarah Beth," Greeley said, but his tone told Slocum that the man cared nothing for his sister. "She is so attentive. Where is she now?"

"It doesn't matter," Slocum said. "You're going to pay for all you've done."

"What? Killing *that*?" Greeley poked the dead Warren Lester with the toe of his fancy boot. "Don't tell me you wouldn't have cut him down if the chance had presented itself. I only used science to accomplish what you didn't with brute force."

"You tasted killing when you blew up Allen back in Sage Junction and you liked it. No more, Greeley, no more. Your killing spree ends here."

"Call me the Dynamite Kid. I like that moniker. It suits me."

"Where's the gold you stole from Snell?"

"Oh, that? It didn't amount to all that much. A quarter of what I have here." Greeley put his hand on the crate in the wagon loaded with gold. "I stashed the gold from the Shady Lady Mine not far from where I thought I had removed you from this glorious equation."

"What are you going on about?" Slocum listened to the furor in front of the bank. The multiple explosions had made the police wary, and with good reason.

"Oh, nothing, Slocum, nothing."

Slocum fired—too late. His slug missed Greeley by a foot, and then the side of the bank blasted outward. Hunks of masonry slammed hard into Slocum and knocked him back. He fell, and stared up in time to see the towering brick wall tip over and come crashing down on top of him.

"Get me out!" Slocum shouted. He had fallen into a mud hole in the alley and this had saved him from being crushed, but he couldn't move the bricks stacked on top of him. As if from a distance, he heard excited voices, and knew the police and bank guards had finally discovered the robbery.

"Mercy," said a voice filtering through the tumble of bricks, "are you still alive under there? I saw you try to stop the robbers."

Slocum kicked and got one leg free. By now a half dozen men were working to free him. When he stood, he faced a florid policeman with a whistle dangling from a leather strip around his neck.

"Did you catch him?" asked Slocum. "Lawrence Greeley?"

"Who might that be?"

"The man who set the explosives all around town, the man who robbed the bank." Slocum took a deep breath and then said, "He calls himself the Dynamite Kid."

The cop stiffened at this. "We got a report that was the name of the gussied-up dude with the dynamite."

"It's him," Slocum said, pointing. "He did this to your bank. How much did he get away with?"

"Can't rightly say, but it might be as much as two hundred pounds of gold in bars and coin. The robbers left the paper money and took only specie."

"Warren Lester," Slocum said. "That's the dead outlaw with the hand blown off." He had caused quite a stir. As he dusted himself off, he stared at the wagon tracks in the alleyway.

"We got more fires," said one of the men. "A half dozen. Come on, Jonathon, help us get them put out."

"You wait here, mister," the policeman said to Slocum. "I've got to lend a hand with those new fires."

Slocum waited until the police officer hurried off, then went to find his horse. He had been lucky dismounting where he had. Greeley had blown large craters in the street to create confusion. Eight horses had fallen victim to Greeley's diversion and, if Slocum could tell, more than one of their owners, too. He swung into the saddle and returned to the alley. Greeley couldn't be too far ahead of him.

He trotted along, looking for the wagon tracks. Two hundred pounds wasn't much of a load for such a powerful team, but Greeley wouldn't hurry. He would think he had all the time in the world to escape with half of Salt Lake City going up in flames and all the citizens either in shock or furiously fighting to keep the other half of their town from burning to the ground. It had been an effective—and vicious—diversion.

When Slocum reached the junction in the road, he had to choose whether to head back in the direction of Sage Junction or due west. The dust in the road was too dry to hold a track, so he had to guess. Slocum galloped toward Sage Junction, and within fifteen minutes was rewarded with the sight of a rider leading a pack animal on the road ahead of him. He squinted and shielded his eyes with his hand. If it hadn't been for Greeley's fancy boots, he might have kept riding, hunting for the wagon. Greeley had planned his escape better than Slocum would have thought for a greenhorn.

Where the wagon had gone, he didn't know, but Greeley had dumped it and transferred his loot to a packhorse to make better time. Slocum judged distances and how the road curved before cutting across country to head off Greeley. When the young man topped a rise, Slocum was waiting for him, six-gun drawn and ready.

"Slocum!"

Greeley jerked at his horse's reins and tried to reverse his path. Slocum fired, intending to get him to surrender. What happened startled him. Lawrence Greeley and his horse exploded. Slocum staggered back a pace, then ran to where Greeley's body was sprawled alongside the road. The self-styled Dynamite Kid was dead.

Poking in the remains, Slocum saw that he had hit Greeley's saddlebags where there must have been some of his explosive.

"That'll teach you to handle explosives properly," Slocum said, only then returning his six-gun to its holster. It took the better part of a half hour for him to catch his own spooked horse, load it with the gold, and then lead it back into Salt Lake City. Confusion still flowed around him like a river swollen from spring runoff, but he returned to the bank where the officer who had freed him from the debris was speaking with several men dressed well and looking distraught. Slocum had seen his share of bankers and knew these were the men responsible for the well-being of the Deseret Bank.

"Jonathon," Slocum called. "I've got something for you." He looked at the bankers, who were now irritated at being interrupted. "Might be it's more for them. This is the gold stolen from the bank."

The confusion before had been the product of Greeley's explosives going off all around town. This pandemonium came from bankers slapping Slocum on the back and all of them trying to shake his hand at the same time.

"They didn't want him in their cemetery," Sarah Beth said sadly. She sat on the railroad depot platform, hands working over and around in a nervous knot that tied and untied itself. Her bright blue eyes were bloodshot from crying, and she stared at the platform rather than Slocum.

"I know," he said. The city fathers had insisted that Greeley's remains be buried alongside the road not far from where he had been blown up. In a way, Slocum thought that was more what Greeley would have wanted. Going up in a cloud of death he had caused himself was too good an end. He should have been hanged.

"I don't know how to thank you for what you've done, John. You're too good to me. Really."

"There wasn't much of a reward offered for returning the bank's gold, but I thought you should have it for all you've been through." Slocum did not add that he now considered them even. She had done a great deal to keep his neck from getting stretched. Putting her on a train headed back East was the best thing for both of them.

"Here," she said, handing him a small, bound volume with holes burned in the cover. "I have no need of this."

"What is it?"

"Lawrence's laboratory notes. He recorded everything. I suppose you can figure out how to make his explosive. You can patent it and make a fortune. I can't bear the thought of ever profiting from it myself. That's not the legacy I wanted from Lawrence."

Slocum took it and shook his head. He was no chemist. More than that, he had no desire for anyone to ever possess the secret of Greeley's potent, deadly explosive. Dynamite was plenty good enough.

"There's the train," she said, shooting to her feet. She took a step, then turned, threw her arms around him, and hugged him tightly. He felt her hot tears soaking into his shirt. Then Sarah Beth spun, and was aboard the train before it had completely stopped. It would be some time before the train pulled out, but she wanted to be away from him and all the memories as quickly as possible.

He went down the steps at the end of the platform and started to toss Greeley's notebook away. On impulse, Slocum began leafing through the pages to see what a genius wrote when he thought no one was watching.

He found that part of Greeley's genius lay in recording every detail, no matter how small. The pages were carefully dated, and the one for the day following the Shady Lady Mine robbery was of particular interest. Slocum turned the book around and around and then smiled. Greeley had made a map showing where he had hidden the gold.

Finding the gold by using the map would be a snap. By the time Slocum had dug it up, he could decide whether to keep it for all the trouble he had gone through or to contact Snell and see if there was a reward offered for its return. The old geezer was a likable sort, and Slocum wasn't inclined to steal from him, especially if Windsor had been accused of all the crimes that the mine owner had pinned on Slocum.

He mounted and rode slowly toward the mountains to the east and a trove of hidden gold. There would be plenty of time on the trail for him to decide what to do with the gold when he recovered it.